NIGHTMARE FOR DR. MORELLE

Helping Interpol unmask the big wheel behind an inter-national narcotics-racket, Dr. Morelle himself becomes involved in a train smash with unforeseen results; while his inimitable secretary, Miss Frayle, making a flying dash across the Continent to Dr. Morelle's help, is also caught up in the sinister tangle.

NIGHTMARE FOR DR. MORELLE

Ernest Dudley

·BLACK·
DAGGER
·CRIME·

First published 1960
by
Robert Hale Limited
This edition 1998 by Chivers Press
Published by arrangement with
the author

ISBN 0 7540 8506 6

British Library Cataloguing in Publication Data available

Printed and bound in Great Britain by
Redwood Books, Trowbridge, Wiltshire

Chapter One

THE DARK-SKINNED MAN with the thin black moustache which ran down the sides of his mouth, stretched himself on the shelf-like bed. The dark-skinned man's name was Zarc. He was short and wiry, with narrow coal-black eyes that shifted from side to side beneath their long lashes. He was dressed European-style, fawn duck trousers, soft patent shoes and white cotton shirt. His jacket, hanging on the peg beside the heavily draped doorway was fawn-coloured.

He moved uneasily, but even if the wooden shelf on which he lay had been comfortable he could not have relaxed. He remained taut, tense, watching.

On the bright metal tray beside him was what looked like a large tumbler with a hole in the bottom which covered the little lamp. Its flame sent his distorted shadow cavorting on the wall of the stuffy cubicle. Beside the glass was a shallow bowl containing what might have been dark molasses. Also on the tray was a long knitting-needle.

The dark, treacly stuff that looked like molasses was opium.

The pipe was about two feet in length elaborately carved and inlaid with imitation gold and ivory. The opium was not pushed into the pipe-bowl after the fashion of filling a pipe with tobacco, here there was only a very small aperture. The old Arab who had brought in the pipe had squatted beside Zarc and proceeded to heat the needle-point over the lamp. When it was hot enough he dipped it into the opium. A certain amount stuck to the needle and he held it over the flame again until it bubbled like sealing-wax.

Zarc watched while again and again the Arab, his wizened face completely absorbed, dipped the needle into the bowl of opium and held it over the flame until sufficient collected at the point to roll a small pill. This done he placed it on the opening of the pipe-bowl and pushed the needle through the pill to make a minute hole. Then Zarc took the pipe. He held it over the flame, and as the pill began to smoke and melt into the pipe-hole he inhaled the musty-smelling fumes through the long stem.

He smoked for a long time, feeling little effect. He began to doubt that he was smoking real opium, and thought he would change to a cigarette. He got up to get the packet of cigarettes in his jacket on the peg. When he tried to walk his head was as clear as it had been before he had entered the place, his brain was active, but he found it difficult to keep his balance. His body seemed to belong to someone else who came blundering after him.

The Arab, his head sunk between his hunched shoulders moved close to him. Zarc gave him a nod, there were whispers between them followed by the surreptitious rustle of crisp bank-notes, and Zarc went out into the street, hot and dazzling under the afternoon sun.

The reaction Zarc was experiencing was extraordinary, but not unfamiliar. It was not his first session with the dream-pipe. This sensation as if his head was going in front, while the rest of him, opium-filled and floating after him, barged against walls, and turning a street-corner required tremendous concentration to get his body to go along with him.

Back at his lodgings, instead of succumbing to delight-filled dreams he slept heavily. When he awoke some two hours later, the musty taste of opium still filled his mouth and when he pushed his fingers through his black, greasy hair, they reeked of it. The smell of it on his clothes was so strong he felt obliged to change before going off to keep his appointment.

Half-an-hour later he was in Inspector Alva's office, not far from Baghdad's South Gate. "You're sure that's all you know?" The detective, his thin mouth drawn back over his white teeth glared at him wolfishly.

The dark-skinned man with the narrow, black moustache nodded. The detective facing him across the square-topped, neatly ordered table gave him a non-committal grunt. He turned to the gaunt, saturnine figure of Dr. Morelle, who sat there in an impeccably cut white suit, his chin nudging the handle of his sword-stick.

"I know this," Zarc said, "that you will find the stuff at old Lukka's place. In four-gallon petrol-tins. There are forty tins hidden away. Where, I could not learn, but they are there. They were delivered by two lorries last night. This I was told two hours ago, in the Street of the Caliph."

Lukka, as Inspector Alva explained to Dr. Morelle, had long been suspected by the local Sûreté and the *gendarmerie* across the Syrian border to be a big wheel in the well-organized dope-smuggling ring, which ran the stuff from operational H.Q. some place beyond the poppy-fields on the old caravan-routes to Palmyra. Lukka lived in a white house outside Baghdad on a hillside, from which he had cut down every tree, so no one could approach without being scrutinized. Pressure in certain corrupt political quarters had up till now made him immune from police action.

"But that is all changed," the detective said. "I am curious to know what goes on inside that house," Inspector Alva murmured. "It is time we arranged a visiting-party."

Dr. Morelle accepted his invitation to go along. Zarc, the police-informer, took his money and his departure. Inspector Alva and Dr. Morelle set off in a police-car waiting outside the Sûreté office, a black, dust-veiled Cadillac. Through the market-place and then at a crawl down stench-filled, crowded back alleys, and then the detective spoke sharply to the driver. The Cadillac squealed to a halt outside a high-walled cemetery. A narrow door in the mud wall opened and there was a muttering of Arabic.

In the shadow of the wall was another long, dusty Cadillac. Through the mud wall door appeared half-a-dozen plainclothes-men, who climbed into the waiting police-car. Followed by Inspector Alva's car, it raced off towards the city's outskirts.

"The first time I accepted the invitation," Dr. Morelle was saying, "was, I recall, in the ancient city of the shahs, the former capital of Ispahan." He had been describing to his companion his travels in Persia, when he had smoked opium on several occasions. "A young and most attractive daughter of a certain silk-merchant described in glowing terms the delights she had obtained from the enticements of the poppy." Dr. Morelle smiled reminiscently. "But then the drug was so commonly used among the well-to-do, that it was often served with afternoon tea."

He went on to explain that not wishing to offend his hosts, he never refused to smoke, but always confined himself to a few whiffs. "I found that it did not affect me in the slightest." And, Dr. Morelle continued, in Indo-China he had found that many of the old French colonists were opium-smokers, and appeared healthy enough. "In fact, it seems to me that opium-smoking in the East is so widespread, it is remarkable how few addicts appear seriously affected by it."

"Perhaps it is like drinking," Inspector Alva said. "People can drink all their lives and no harm done."

"Most of us," Dr. Morelle nodded, "possess a tolerance for alcohol which if not over-taxed need produce no serious consequences. Of course, the after-effects of opium might comparably prove more destructive, while the drug itself is more habit-forming than alcohol."

Inspector Alva ordered his driver to drop back to avoid the yellow dust-cloud swirled up by the Cadillac ahead. They had turned off the made-up road on to a dusty track which wound its way up an incline, rock-cluttered and barren. To the right of the track the terrain dropped down to a narrow valley, and across it, on the rising hillside stood Lukka's white house in magnificent isolation. A low wall could be seen in the sun-glare surrounding the grounds and outbuildings. The green vegetation stood out in the arid landscape; where the gardens were bared by the cut-down trees, windows glinted in the shadowed balconies.

The first Cadillac had arrived, parked beneath a cluster of palms, a hundred yards from the gates of the house. Inspector Alva's Cadillac passed the crowded car and climbed the hillside; the gates swung open as if at the touch of a button, and the car disappeared into a walled courtyard of the white villa. A few minutes later, Alva's driver came back through the gates and gave the signal. The plainclothes-policemen raced to the house.

The old man, Lukka, made a picture of insensate evil with his white, flowing moustache, pointed beard and yellow goat's eyes. He bossed his servants with a crackling whip, cursing at them to obey no orders but his. Rounding them up, the police began their search.

Throughout that afternoon the men searched. There was not a sign of the petrol tins that Zarc had been so certain were cached there. Lukka spat in Inspector Alva's face and refused to talk; the servants, in cringing fear of him dare not and would not co-operate with the police. Inspector Alva, perspiring and grating his white teeth with frustration, was almost prepared to admit defeat.

During all the activity and the noisy hubbub, Dr. Morelle found himself alone. He drifted out of the house into the luxurious gardens where gardeners worked to keep them green and blooming, and took a sandstone path to some outbuildings. They were long, low and windowless, the sunlight shafting into their shadowy corners through wide archways.

Dr. Morelle moved through a series of compartments, store-rooms or deserted servants' quarters. His stick rapped the floor and now and again against the thick walls. No hiding-places, no cavities were revealed. At the end of one low building were stables, which Dr. Morelle at first thought were also deserted. Then he came to a stall occupied by a mare and her foal. He stood admiring the beautiful white Arab and derived some faint amusement from the foal's unsteady antics. Suddenly it seemed to shy and plunge fearfully; to Dr. Morelle's ears came a sharp metallic sound. The foal had kicked against something in the straw.

Dr. Morelle dragged at his cigarette, his eyes narrowed. A minute or two later he was back in the house and speaking to Inspector Alva.

The Sûreté detective with three of his men accompanied Dr. Morelle to the stables. The mare and foal were led out, the straw was pushed back from the stall floor, a section of which was revealed and was lifted by a steel ring. It was the ring the foal had caught with his hoof.

The underground store-room beneath was stacked with petrol tins. One after another was hoisted up and policemen ripped them apart. Inside each was a cellophane-wrapped sticky mess of brown treacly substance that gave off a musty odour.

It was raw opium.

Three-quarters of a ton of it was lifted out of the subterranean hiding-place. Lukka yelled and cursed, spat and cracked his whip, protested his innocence and utter ignorance of the secret cache; but it got him nowhere. He was placed under arrest and taken off. A police guard was left at the house and arrangements were made to shift the opium to Baghdad.

Some two hours later, back at the Sûreté office Dr. Morelle was sipping coffee, taking care not to lift the cup in his left hand, with Inspector Alva, who was reaching the end of an effusive flow of gratitude. "A superb piece of detective-work, Dr. Morelle," he said. *"Magnifique, formidable."*

"I was dubious about the house itself being the hiding-place," Dr. Morelle said. "The outbuildings and stables were empty, so that when I saw one stall of the stables occupied, it occurred to me that it might have some significance."

"The old devil had cleared out that part to ensure that none of his servants could learn of the hidden stuff."

Dr. Morelle nodded, and returned his coffee-cup to the tray on the desk. "I instance it as merely further evidence of the human sub-conscious compulsion to reveal his innermost secrets," Dr. Morelle said. "It would be curious, were it not so common in my experience, how consistently a criminal will deliberately, if by some oblique means, draw attention to his misdeed."

"You are referring to the mare and foal Lukka left behind in the stall?" Inspector Alva's tone was faintly dubious. "But surely that was to throw dust in the eyes of anyone suspecting what lay hidden under the straw?"

"That was his conscious intention, no doubt; but sub-consciously he felt impelled to leave some object which would betray him, and what more likely than a restless foal which would kick against the very object which marked his secret."

"You believe less in Fate—*Kismet*—then, Dr. Morelle, than in a man's own motives?"

Dr. Morelle smiled thinly, "What is *Kismet*," he said, "but the promptings of one's own innermost conscience which cries out that the guilty must bring about his own punishment, the destroyer encompass his self-destruction, the murderer incur his own death?"

The other glanced at him penetratingly and gave a shrewd nod. "You apply your mind as one who has made himself familiar with the philosophy of this part of the world," he said.

Dr. Morelle shrugged as if to hint that he was far from unfamiliar with all the philosophies of the globe. "Who could resist applying that knowledge to the evidence offered me in this afternoon's situation by the presence of the Arab mare and her foal?"

"It certainly shook old Lukka," the detective said. "If looks could kill, you wouldn't be chatting with me now over a cup of coffee."

"And to have missed such excellent coffee would have been especially tragic," Dr. Morelle said smoothly.

The other was about to reply suitably, when the telephone on his desk rang, and with an apology to Dr. Morelle he picked up the receiver. Dr. Morelle turned to gaze idly out of the window over the sun-dried and yellow brick buildings, silhouetted like cut-out stage scenery against the translucid light of the late afternoon sky.

Chapter Two

"IRAQUI SÛRETÉ." Inspector Alva spoke quickly and in low tones and after a few moments replaced the receiver. Dr. Morelle turned as he heard him say: "Our C.I.D. chief presents his compliments, and asks if you might care to accompany me to Al Raschid Street."

"A further development?" Dr. Morelle said.

"It would appear so."

The black, dust-smeared Cadillac was at the door when Dr. Morelle and Inspector Alva came out, and they drove towards Al Raschid Street; at the broad New Street the car turned northward. Inspector Alva appeared preoccupied with his own thoughts, while Dr. Morelle eyed the passing street scene. He found himself reflecting wryly on Miss Frayle's ideas of Baghdad which for her, far away in London, had conjured up visions of romance and mystery. She had talked enthusiastically of graceful minarets and bright-tiled domes, all the exotic fables surrounding Haroun el Raschid.

As the Cadillac sped through the city, its dilapidated relics, its squalid alleys and the gusty shamal blowing from the north-west and dusting the streets, offered themselves for view in all their unromantic reality.

Dr. Morelle's thoughts turned to the raid on Lukka's place; and then his mind's eye switched to those acre upon acre of poppy-fields just across the not far distant

Persian border from Khanagen, which he had seen glistening white under the burning sun; sown in November in the rich, loose earth they would ripen for picking by February next and yield their crop of opium.

Dr. Morelle's reflections now turned to London; to the third floor of the impressively undecorative seven-storied white stone block, overlooking the Embankment, New Scotland Yard, and once more he was striding along the corridor to an office which commands the best view in London of the Whitehall entrance to Downing Street. Here, where the walls are charted with diagrams of Interpol's radio links and maps of member nations, he had spent lengthy talks with British Interpol officers.

And his mind turned to another office at the French Ministry of the Interior, 60 Boulevard Gouvion St. Cyr, Paris, a long, rectangular block, its mouse-coloured façade grim as any prison, with two gendarmes ever watchful on its steps. This was Interpol's headquarters, its offices bursting with criminal-dossiers and records; cabinets crammed with every aspect of counterfeiting and drug-trafficking, fraud and confidence trickery cases; individual police documentation; and a vast library on English, French, German, Spanish and Italian criminal psychology, graphology, criminal tactics, medical studies of insanity and criminal responsibility, toxicology, finger-printing systems, psychiatry, sexology, forensic medicine or C.I.D. histories, plus police journals and magazines.

Here Dr. Morelle had talked to the specialists, tucked away at their desks and files in odd corners. Here, at 60 Boulevard Gouvion and at Scotland Yard he had encountered the impulse which had sparked him off for Baghdad and points east; the region that was the main morphine supply-source for the West Europe narcotic-traffickers.

It was no self-appointed task, there had been unofficial hints that his active interest in the subject would not be unwelcome, and behind the implied invitation lay the shrewd notion that where orthodox means had failed, those more unorthodox might succeed. What still nagged Interpol's pride and mocked its power was the fact that there remained a boss of one octopus-like narcotics racket still operating, the tentacles under his control still spread through Europe and the Middle East, reaching out to America. This was a challenge that must be met and wiped out.

So far only the small fry had been caught, those who hadn't been eliminated before the police got on to them, to make them sing. The man at the top was without mercy or scruples. The way to the boss was not short or easy, and it must prove dangerous. Dr. Morelle had started along the dark path at a point where the trafficking began and ended. He had witnessed the spectacle of the poppy-fields bending gently before a breeze from the desert; he had observed at the end of the line the dreamy opium-smokers happy in the grip of the end-product.

Dr. Morelle had been fortunate at the Baghdad stage of his quest, his search *en route* had produced little that was tangible, vague leads East; but now he was experiencing direct action in a case which he had no doubt was included in those ramifications that claimed his probing interest.

A native policeman waved the Cadillac through the traffic, past fierce-looking bearded Arab chiefs surrounded by bodyguards bristling with daggers and pistols; the hideously maimed and whining blind, the innumerable beggars, hawkers and street-merchants, and ordinary men and women hurrying to their homes. It was evening and the muezzins on the city's hundred mosques were calling the faithful prayer :

"Allahu Akbar;
I testify that there is no god but Allah,
I testify that Mohammed is the prophet of Allah.
Come to prayer,
Come to good works.
Allahu Akbar;
There is no god but Allah."

The Cadillac neared the North Gate, Dr. Morelle could see the blue dome of the Great Mosque, where no unbeliever had ever entered, and idly he wondered if he would be allowed inside the thirteenth-century place of worship on Al Raschid Street to which he was going. As he tried to recall various details of Moslem etiquette, the car suddenly swung off the main street into a narrow, winding lane overhung by latticed windows.

The picture of progressive decay and squalid poverty became increasingly vivid and overpowering; the flat and angled roofs of the buildings reaching towards each other and throwing the outlines of doors and windows and cellar-steps into uninviting shadow. It was not a salubrious quarter, dark figures moved in and out of sinister doorways; not a place for the unwary to linger unarmed or without a guard.

The car drove slowly, but without a halt, and then

B

they were in Al Raschid Street, the driver pulling up close behind another car parked alongside an entrance to the ancient mosque that for centuries had been slowly crumbling away. Dark and gloomy, it was nothing like a shrine at Kazimain that Dr. Morelle remembered for its minarets of coloured tiles and twin domes sheeted in pure gold.

An Arab police-officer stepped out of the mosque doorway and saluted the detective who, with Dr. Morelle got out of the Cadillac and went towards the other car, and the man standing close by it. His uniform was meticulously pressed and his hair beneath his peaked cap was close-cropped and grizzled. This was the chief of the C.I.D., an ex-army colonel, from whom had come the telephone-call to Inspector Alva's office.

The colonel greeted Dr. Morelle with respectful warmth. They had dined together the previous night, and exchanged views and pooled information on the dope-racket. The former had laid particular emphasis upon the implacable ruthlessness of the set-up with which they were dealing, warning Dr. Morelle with deadly seriousness of the grim danger he ran by pursuing the course he had set for himself. Now, he said in perfect English: "In case you imagined I might have over-stressed the personal peril in which you have placed yourself, I thought you should see for yourself the sort of thing you are up against."

He turned to Inspector Alva murmuring something in Arabic, and then gave a nod at the Arab police-officer hovering close by.

The policeman led the way along the side of the building to another door recessed in the mosque-wall.

The spot was dark and evil-smelling and the Arab stopped and pointed to the figure who lay there, face upward.

He was dead. The face was of a dark-skinned man and a thin, black moustache curved down towards a blood-stained chin.

"Zarc." Inspector Alva muttered the name unemotionally; it was as if he was not in the least surprised at what he saw.

"A not entirely unfamiliar method of dealing with an informer," the colonel said.

As his eyes grew accustomed to the dim light, Dr. Morelle caught the glint of a knife beside the body. It was stained with blood, and next to it lay a pinky-red object.

"A tongue," Inspector Alva said in Dr. Morelle's ear. "His tongue."

Chapter Three

THE COOL, spring night was enfolding Paris when the Air France Super Constellation touched down at Orly Airport. Perimeter and runway lights stabbed the dusk, and the glare of light from the reception and Customs block spilled over the disembarking passengers as they made their way from the plane for baggage and passport checks.

Dr. Morelle was passed through with the speed and lack of formality given an important passenger whose arrival was expected, which helpful deference he accepted with his usual outward show of indifference. Within fifteen minutes he was outside and stepping into the chauffeur-driven limousine sent to await him, and was being whisked off to Paris.

A few hours ago he had been enduring the hot and stuffy atmosphere of Baghdad, the sun brazenly beating down from a copper sky; now here he was heading silently through the clear air towards the welcoming glitter of Paris at night.

However far away behind him he had put Iraq's garish capital in terms of time and distance, it was still realistically close to Dr. Morelle in the shape of his thoughts clustered tight about the recollection of the previous afternoon and Zarc's murder in the shadow of that evil-smelling corner of the Blue Mosque. The killer had left behind nothing that might put the police on his trail, the only lead being the opium-den where Zarc had picked up the tip-off concerning Lukka; but inquiries had yielded nothing useful up till the time Dr. Morelle had left for Paris.

The grim symbol of the cut-out tongue took the Baghdad Sûreté no further along the dark road towards unmasking the identity of the top man behind the dope-ring. But Dr. Morelle's interest was no longer focused on this part of the world; Paris held more promise for him. Here was his next source of information and leads. Europe was the mainspring of the illegal narcotics operation, of this he was already fully aware.

The quiet little hotel off the Place de Rivoli was one Dr. Morelle had chosen with the object of attracting as little attention to himself as possible. He was uncertain of the length of his stay, but his coming and going amid the plush surroundings of a busier and luxury hotel would have aroused immediate interest on the part of newspapermen, and others with an even stronger speculative interest in the reasons behind his visit. The porter took his baggage and took it to the lift. There was a message for him at reception. Dr. Morelle glanced at it. It was a telephone number which indicated the most fashionable part of Paris. That was all the message said.

In his room, Dr. Morelle held the slip of paper over the flame of his cigarette-lighter and watched it crumble into the ashtray.

After a bath and dinner, a lamb chop with mushrooms, and a half-bottle of claret, served in his room Dr. Morelle phoned down for a taxi and presently he was heading in the direction of the Fauberg Saint-Germain. His destination was a house in the Rue de Bellechasse, which runs up from the Seine and cuts across the Rue Saint-Dominique.

The taxi drew up outside a house discreetly withdrawn from the wide street, beyond tall railings; from her first-floor apartment whose ornately ornamented balconies overlooked the quiet garden Madame Babette supplied her exclusive, upper-crust male clientele with their varied libidinous requirements.

As Dr. Morelle came into the exquisitely furnished room, with its thick white wall-to-wall carpet and subtly pervasive scent, the tall, svelte woman crossed from the writing-desk and held out her hands to him.

"Why do you not come to Paris more often?" she said.

He gave her a quizzical smile as he took her hands in his. Dark haired with wide-apart, luminous eyes, she was so beautifully made up that in the richly subdued light she looked no more than in her thirties; the writing-desk, Dr. Morelle knew, held the code-names of members of some of Europe's best-known families, husbands, and fathers, politicians and literary lights, artists and film-stars and big-business tycoons.

Over coffee and fabulous Napoleon brandy, with a bouquet which Dr. Morelle's aquiline nose had not known for some time, they chatted casually, the undertones of past days breaking the surface of their conversation. Madame Babette reminded him of a night when she had fallen to her knees before him, her voice choked with the anguish that had wracked her.

" 'You are taking the cure,' you said to me; do you remember? I can hear your words now. 'Here,' you said; 'Now'."

"The Cold Turkey," he said, through the smoke of his long Corona-Corona.

His mind went back to the scene. "Make me take it," she had begged him. "Make me kill this monkey on my back." She had preferred it that way. Get the agony over with as quickly as possible. The heroin which had her in its claw would be withdrawn at once, and, if she lived, she would be cured in five days. She would not go to a sanatorium.

Dr. Morelle had put her to bed. It had not been such a magnificent bedroom in those days; the skids had been under Madame Babette. Her addiction had taken as heavy a toll of the profits of her trade as it had sapped her physical strength and will-power. When the time came for her shot, the cure proper had begun. He was recalling the twisted smile she had given him, "Better clear the sharp things out of here," she had told him. It was the last time she smiled for some time.

He had sat with her while she lay on the bed waiting for the moment when the longing for the heroin kick would seize her; she kept looking towards the clock on the bedside table. As the hands crept slowly up and down its face she began twisting restlessly from side to side on the bed. Then she got up and went and stood by the window, then began to pace the bedroom up and down aimlessly.

About four p.m. the yawning began. She yawned and stretched for the next two hours, long shuddering yawns which racked her lovely, slim body. Dr. Morelle remembered how he had yawned with her. Then she had begun to shiver and complain she was chilled to the bone. The horror closed in; she was unable to remain still a moment. She wrapped herself up in blankets and lying on her stomach, she would then jerk upright, throw herself over on her back, arching herself, moaning and gasping.

Now she had begun to plead with him, frothing at the mouth. She dragged herself from the bed to start her interminable pacing, head down between her hunched shoulders. Like some wild, cat-like animal she turned on Dr. Morelle, cursing him because of the cold, then crying out that the bedroom was stifling.

As the dawn filtered past the curtains, her skin turned blue, great weals appeared and swelled so that it had the look of a turkey's flesh. Cold Turkey. She fell into a coma-like sleep, breathing as if she was suffering from a severe head-cold. When she awoke suddenly, two hours later, Dr. Morelle had a raving madwoman on his hands.

She felt that she was suffocating; she sneezed violently, sobbed and choked; she threw herself out of bed and lay on the floor, her legs threshing. She was becoming badly bruised. "I'm frozen—frozen," she kept screaming at Dr. Morelle. It was a hot Paris mid-summer and Dr. Morelle had all the room's heating on. Then she tried to force open the window and throw herself out, and she fought off Dr. Morelle so ferociously that he was forced to stun her with a Judo blow.

She was violently sick, screaming all the time that she was poisoned. Over and over as that morning wore on she fought, clawed and bit Dr. Morelle. He would hold her in his arms till she was worn out temporarily, then he would put her back to bed. All the time he talked to her quietly and gently, and watching him she took his hand and grasped it as if she would never let go. Then the screaming and fighting would start over again. Perspiration soaked her night-dress and the bed-clothes: None of the servants who ran her house would come near her; Dr. Morelle had to change her; she had to be bathed and he carried her to and from the bathroom.

The dreadful struggle went on for three days. She became skeleton-thin, her face was swollen. She wouldn't eat; drinking only water which Dr. Morelle gave her. On the fourth day, early in the morning, he had to gag her with bandages to stop her from biting her lips until the blood came. But she was lying absolutely still. All that day she stayed quiet. Dr. Morelle sat beside her that evening and throughout the night, checking her resources and making sure that she had the physical strength and mental guts to stick it out. Towards dawn he keeled over in a chair and fell asleep.

When he awoke, he found her staring at him from the bed, her hand pale and blue-veined thin, clinging to his. *"Merci ... merci. ..."*

It was over. Madame Babette was no longer a drug-addict.

"You know," she was saying to him now, "you never really explained why you did what you did for me."

He glanced at her. Her eyes were warm and smiling. "You mean because you were what you were?"

"And what I am."

"I was and am a doctor before anything else. You were in need of my help and what skill I had to offer."

"And you have never made me feel as if I have——" She broke off and took in the luxurious room with a look "—as if I failed you by not changing my profession."

His profile as his gaze rested on the writing-table was enigmatic. She gave a sharp sigh, and he said without looking at her: "It is not my role to pass judgment on your morals. Besides, you forget you once risked your life for me."

She shrugged. "That little business," she said. "It was nothing."

"It would have meant a bullet in my back if your warning had failed to reach me."

"How can I help you this time?" she said abruptly.

He drew at his cigar and began telling her of the reasons that during the past few weeks had sent him half across the world and back. Madame Babette's eyes became veiled, her expression guarded. Her voice was lowered as they talked together for another hour, although her contribution to the topic was cryptic and her tenseness became more and more evident; the barrier that had somehow begun to creep up between them like a sheet of glass grew high and increasingly impenetrable.

He took a last sip of brandy and stood there in his dark grey single-breasted suit, his face gaunt and tanned above the impeccable cream silk shirt and knitted tie. The grey at his temples caught the light so that the raven blackness of his hair made a vivid contrast. He glanced at his thin gold wrist-watch. "I have another rendezvous. Not so pleasurable as this; it is with a man named Rommerque."

Her long, heavy eyelashes flickered.

"The *flic*?"

He nodded; the idle thought flashed across his mind that Inspector Rommerque's name figured on Madame Babette's list. Not that he felt any concern for the detective's morals, either. He had met up with Rommerque during his last visit to Paris *en route* to the Middle East, and retained the impression of a swarthy, plump man with a somewhat mysterious air, and appropriately secretive manner of speech, as if he felt himself in constant danger of being overheard.

Some twenty minutes later Dr. Morelle was in Inspector Rommerque's cramped office at the *Police Judicaire*, a grim-looking building on the Quai des Orfevres, whose harsh outlines were shrouded by the haze rising from the Seine.

Rommerque had greeted him with a knowing wink and cryptic news that he had a car waiting in which he invited Dr. Morelle to accompany him right away on a dash some distance out.

In the speeding Renault, Rommerque opened up sufficiently to explain that their destination was a heroin factory, thirty kilometres south of Paris. "One of the small illegal production units that we know to be part of the main organization." He chuckled smugly. "I allow it to continue for the time being. It can be of some assistance, until I have run the mainspring down." He laughed out loud at his own joke.

Again that idle flash across Dr. Morelle's thoughts that the man beside him was not unknown to the elegant, scented apartment which he had not long left in the Rue de Bellechasse; and now it occurred to him to wonder how the detective could afford to be on Madame Babette's list, on the relatively meagre sort of payroll he must get at the Quai des Orfevres.

"It is the only way," he heard Inspector Rommerque say, "I have to keep a foot in the enemy's camp. Not a

policeman's foot, you understand? I am a client, a
buyer. To-night, I am bringing a friend who is interested."

Dr. Morelle murmured understandingly.

"Another small cog, you understand?" the other's
hands spread in a throw-away movement. "But you
shall see."

The place they arrived at suggested from the outside
a disused garage. There was nothing to excite attention,
no smoke or smells, no sign of activity. Inspector Rommerque muttered something to the driver who stayed
where he was, as he got out of the car, then, followed by
Dr. Morelle, made his way in the darkness to a small
door set in big double doors. There was some unlocking,
noises of bolts being drawn, the small door opened.
Shadowy figures, whisperings, and the detective and Dr.
Morelle were admitted.

The first thing Dr. Morelle noticed was the odour;
while men in masks moved about what looked like a
cross between a wash-house and a laboratory, the smell
of the opium simmering in small-size vats was penetrat-
ing and acrid. Inspector Rommerque was coughing and
blinking. The masked men were the chemists and their
assistants, and the working-hands carrying and cleaning
and repairing. They wore rubber gloves and overalls,
some also wore goggles. Their entire appearance made
an eerie impression.

"Brewing and transforming liquid opium can be devil-
ish nasty," Inspector Rommerque said in Dr. Morelle's
ear. "A drop can mean a bad burn, and the stuff is
always bubbling and spurting."

They were working to a schedule of heroin production

per diem, Inspector Rommerque explained. Some heroin factories, it seemed preferred to receive the first opium derivative, base black heroin, for conversion into heroin. Dr. Morelle knew how three kilos of the stuff could be smuggled through in a flannel belt, and he deduced that the opium here was delivered at the door from Istanbul. The detective at his side was saying: "More involved and riskier that way than if they went on to black morphine direct. Has to be far more gear, too."

To Dr. Morelle there seemed to be gadgets all over the place, including a radio-set. There were laboratory filters and glass globes and strainers and bottles of acids. In one corner were stacked valises. The opium arrived in these.

Dr. Morelle watched two white-coated, masked men standing before a large basin of brownish liquid on the boil. The opium had to be entirely reduced, and it took seven hours. This was where protection was necessary. To one side stood the biggest vat half-filled with previously boiled liquid now cooling off.

The boiling substance was yellowish and gaseous; now and then a great golden bubble would rise to the surface and burst, but the cooling stuff resembled thickish mud.

During the next stage Dr. Morelle noted the use to which the radio was put. The cooled-off liquid had to be filtered by means of an electric dynamo, and to muffle the vibrating sound of the dynamo the radio was tuned in to the loudest possible music. Doors and windows were closed, though special ventilators had been fitted to the place. Dr. Morelle observed the mixture being combined with certain acids and refiltered, until the first derivative, black morphine was produced.

"Takes twenty hours to turn this into heroin," Inspector Rommerque said. "When there's an alarm, first thing they do is draw the furnace and get rid of the opium. If opium is found, they can collect up to two years."

When Dr. Morelle had seen all there was to see, he and the detective left. The doors were locked behind them, and Dr. Morelle paused to look back at the unimpressive building. It gave no hint of the nefarious activities within. He followed Inspector Rommerque to the Renault and they drove off through the darkness.

Chapter Four

THEY WERE on the outskirts of Paris approaching a cross-roads, when Inspector Rommerque spoke to the driver, who slowed the Renault with a squeal of tyres and made a sharp turn left. The detective in his mysterious voice, spoke out of the side of his mouth to Dr. Morelle.

"I think we should not conclude this evening's little entertainment without some action," he said. He patted the region beneath his breast-pocket, and Dr. Morelle could see the bulge indicative of a pistol in its holster. "We are going to a wily bird, named Carrin," the other was saying. "He is the boss of the heroin factory you have just seen; not a big wheel, you understand, but another cog in this dope-trafficking machinery. To-night perhaps I will put him behind bars; I have given him enough rope."

Dr. Morelle caught Inspector Rommerque's smile in the darkness, and decided he was playing up his secret important role, while he was forced to concede that the detective possessed a remarkable aptitude, backed up by nonchalant courage and initiative, for being able to move inside the enemy's camp.

Here he was now, confidently moving in on the boss of the factory himself.

"I will explain that I have come direct from the factory," Inspector Rommerque said, "and want to make a back-door deal for heroin. You will see how greedily the small fry fall over themselves for cash."

The car turned through some iron gates and up a tree-shaded drive that was a tunnel under the moonless night sky. From under the trees they drew up at a flight of steps running down from a pillared porch.

As they got out of the car Dr. Morelle looked around him, but there was no sign of life in the darkness, the house might have been deserted. He followed Rommerque to the front door and they waited, listening to the faint buzz of the door-bell within. The Renault's driver had joined them, making a massive bulk in the shadows.

The door opened and Rommerque spoke to someone inside. They were invited into the large square parquet-floored hall with a wide centre staircase. They stood there watching the wiry little man who had admitted them vanish into a double-doored room opposite. In a few moments he re-appeared, and Inspector Rommerque and Dr. Morelle, with the driver hovering behind them found themselves in a large ornately furnished library that ran practically the depth of the house, with, at one end a wide desk in front of floor to ceiling curtained windows.

From behind the desk a thin man in his early sixties, came forward. He nodded to the wiry individual who went out and closed the doors.

This was Carrin. Inspector Rommerque said to him coolly : "I have had the pleasure of doing business with your organization. He waved a hand at Dr. Morelle. "A friend of mine, also interested in what you supply."

Carrin eyed Dr. Morelle narrowly, then turned to

Inspector Rommerque. "I do not do business without an appointment normally," he said doubtfully.

"Perhaps you would care to check with your factory?" the detective said affably. "They know me there. And that I am known to your top man." He nodded towards the telephone on the writing-desk, and mentioned a number.

Carrin hesitated, rubbing the tip of a pointed nose reflectively. Then he gave a shrug. "You know the price?" Inspector Rommerque muttered affirmatively, and the thin man crossed to a section of the bookshelves running along the wall. He seemed to press somewhere along a shelf, whereupon the array of books swung out into the room, noiselessly. Carrin moved behind the book-shelf section, and after a moment re-appeared, with a flat, brown-paper package in his hand.

"Show me the colour of your money," he said.

The detective stared at the package, then at the man holding it. The next moment he had made a lightning-like movement, and the bulge in the region of his breast-pocket vanished; the pistol appeared in his hand, aimed at Carrin's stomach. It was a Bernardelli .25, glinting unpleasantly, and Dr. Morelle wished it had been a hand-filling police-revolver instead, a Smith and Wesson, for example. Automatics weren't so dependable. But the Bernardelli scared the wits out of Carrin, all right. Inspector Rommerque's voice was calm, his words off-hand. "I place you, Pierre Carrin, under immediate arrest, as a confirmed and dangerous narcotics trafficker."

Carrin had wilted like a dahlia in a black frost. Recalling the scene afterwards, Dr. Morelle realized it held an air of unreality, like an excerpt from some cheap melodrama; but that was the way Inspector Rommerque played it. He closed in, whipping out a pair of hand-cuffs, and as one bracelet clicked on Carrin's wrist, he gave a yelp and tore into the detective tooth and claw, but he subsided under a slap down from the Bernardelli over his ear.

The door opened and the small, wiry man stood there irresolutely. The police-car driver dealt with him expertly, another pair of handcuffs clicked and then there came the sound of running footsteps and the slamming of a door, followed by the harsh acceleration of a car driving off. It was later on that it was learned that two members of Carrin's little crowd had effected a get-away.

Inspector Rommerque and his driver made a quick search of the villa, Dr. Morelle himself checking documents found in the writing-desk and wall-safe, while Carrin and his accomplice, handcuffed to each other, watched with a bitter gaze. The driver, who had been looking over the house returned for a brief, quiet talk with Inspector Rommerque, who nodded, and with a glance at the handcuffed pair picked up the telephone. The massive driver turned to Dr. Morelle.

"Two of them have got away," he muttered. "A girl named Celeste Ruz and a man whose identity we do not know. Took a Peugeot, and headed for Paris."

Inspector Rommerque had got through to the Quai des Orfevres and was speaking incisively. He replaced the receiver, smiled confidently at Dr. Morelle, and marched out of the library.

When the detective came in a few minutes later he

expressed his surprise at what he had found. In the cellar, a plant for purifying morphine and converting it into heroin; other apparatus, an electric vacuum pump and electric pulverizer; together with huge quantities of heroin, raw opium and morphine.

Dr. Morelle drove back to the building overlooking the Seine with Inspector Rommerque, who was received with the news that Celeste Ruz had been caught. She was alone, having dropped the man when she had eluded the police-car chasing her. The detective sent for her.

Dr. Morelle saw a tall, big-boned girl with a well-developed figure. Long black hair, dark, brilliant eyes, pinched yet finely chiselled features, the cheek bones high; and her small red mouth would have been pretty except for the twitching at the corners. She paced the narrow office like a caged wild cat.

Inspector Rommerque gently suggested she saved her energy. For a moment she sat down and stared at Dr. Morelle.

"Who is he?"

"Dr. Morelle. He is interested in this very nasty business you and I have to talk over."

Dr. Morelle thought that in the girl's half-tamed, flashing eyes he denoted a glimmer of appeal.

"Listen," Inspector Rommerque said to her, as she got to her feet again, resuming her cat-like prowl. "You shall have a little present. You know I always think of you."

He pulled a shallow drawer in the battered old desk. From it he took a small, flat white paper packet, which he carefully opened. Gleaming white dust trickled out.

The light in the girl's eyes was that of someone dying of thirst in the desert and sees a mirage.

"Gently." The detective smiled at her encouragingly. "Tell me who he was, and where did you leave him?"

Dr. Morelle watched her, as she stood rigid, silent, her hands clenched, staring down at the floor. Slowly her face lifted to the white dust which Inspector Rommerque was allowing to run gently up and down on the broad blade of a paper-knife.

"Not so much to ask," he insinuated softly. "Sooner or later he will be caught and you will have suffered your anguish for nothing."

The girl's mouth trembled, her white teeth fastened over her underlip. Suddenly she burst into tears. She stood weeping, uncontrollably. The detective moved round to her and gently eased her into the chair. He waited until the violent sobs had been exhausted.

She choked out a name, the tears still streaming down her face. Without any sign of hurry Inspector Rommerque threw Dr. Morelle a smug little smile, sat down again and scribbled on the huge, untidy blotter before him. He nodded to himself and then threw the white packet across the desk. Celeste Ruz pounced on it.

"Look where this stuff takes you," she rasped at Dr. Morelle. "I never thought that one day I'd give away my lover for it."

"Lovers should not be difficult to come by," the detective said calmly. He moved to her and went with her to the door. "This time," he said, "you go free, but we watch and wait, you understand? Next time, the only reward may be a prison-cell."

She had gone without a glance at Dr. Morelle. The

detective came back into the room, slowly shaking his head. "What can you do? I have tried to help her in the past." He spread his hands helplessly. "Now it has reached the stage where I can do no more than take advantage of her addiction."

Dr. Morelle shrugged with a show of indifference. It was Inspector Rommerque's method and no affair of his. It certainly seemed to achieve results which so far as the other was concerned was all that mattered.

"No doubt," he said, "she is more useful to you free than locked up."

An hour later, Dr. Morelle was back in his comfortable room at the hotel, relaxing with a large whisky and soda and dragging thoughtfully at a Le Sphinx. It was after eleven o'clock.

It had been quite an evening for him.

His thoughts returned again to Madame Babette. Her evident fear when he had begun questioning her about the object of his presence in Paris. Odd that a woman of her profession and her character should be too scared to talk, even to him. She owed more to him than any man, he had saved her from the abyss. And then his mind's eye flickered back to the scene outside the mosque in Al Raschid Street, the sprawled figure in the shadows.

Was he, he wondered as he took a drink, on the right road? Every move he made was taking him a step further into the underworld of traffickers in drugs and addicts, but was he drawing closer to the man at the top? He began thinking about Carrin and the audacious manner in which Inspector Rommerque had dealt with him, though he felt that the detective's action had been prompted largely by the wish to impress. Dr. Morelle had to admit that unusual as his methods were they produced results. There came to his mind the scene in the office at the Quai des Orfevres, and then the telephone on the bedside-table rang.

He thought it was probably Inspector Rommerque.

He crossed the room and lifted the receiver. It was a husky, woman's voice on the line.

"Dr. Morelle?"

"Who is that?"

"This is Celeste—Celeste Ruz. Can I see you to-night? It is important."

Chapter Five

Out of the corner of his eye, Dr. Morelle was aware of the man with the white wavy hair and the gardenia, at the other end of the bar taking another keen look at him.

This was the rendezvous suggested by Celeste Ruz over the telephone less than half-an-hour earlier; Dr. Morelle had arrived expecting to find her waiting. But she had not shown up. The bar was not very busy, and the minutes ticked by as Dr. Morelle drank a whisky and soda and dragged at a cigarette.

He was reflecting that the girl had sounded calm and sure of herself over the phone. She had given no hint of what lay behind her urgent appeal that they should meet; but he had presumed that it concerned her own desperate situation. Perhaps she went in fear of her life as did others who had turned police-informers. If it was his help she wanted, he wondered why she failed to show.

It was then that he had noticed the white-haired man's interest in him. Now, he was experiencing the feeling that at any moment the stranger was going to approach him.

Sure enough the man drained his glass, and with a half-smile edged slowly along the bar. Dr. Morelle eyed him stonily. He was a prematurely old man, whose features had at one time been clear-cut and handsome, but which were now heavily lined, with a sag to his mouth and his eyes had a half-glazed look. He was of medium height, of slim build and expensively dressed; Dr. Morelle observed the diamond tie-clip, and the gold ring. He paused in front of Dr. Morelle, looking up at him with a friendly smile.

"Have I the pleasure of speaking to Dr. Morelle?"

"You have," Dr. Morelle said.

"I am a friend of Celeste Ruz."

Dr. Morelle regarded him narrowly. Was this some sort of trap the girl had prepared for him?

"Will you have a drink?" the other said. "My name is De Goury."

Dr. Morelle indicated that his own glass was still half-full. The man appeared friendly enough and no doubt would offer some explanation for the Ruz girl's absence.

De Goury called for a brandy for himself.

"After phoning you," he said to Dr. Morelle, "Celeste apparently got some notion that meeting you here might be dangerous."

"For whom?"

The man who called himself De Goury suddenly looked at Dr. Morelle humourlessly. The half-glazed eyes held a sinister quality, as if they had stared into the bottomless depths of evil. "You are interested in the dope-racket?"

"What is that to do with you?"

"You are right to be cautious," the white-haired man said. He took his brandy from the olive-skinned, white-jacketed barman. His voice had lowered. He glanced into his glass, but did not drink. "Celeste sent this message. She will meet you in Hamburg the day after to-morrow. But not here in Paris. Hamburg."

"I heard what you said."

"You could take the Nord Express to-morrow evening," De Goury said, and took a gulp of brandy. "Pleasant journey," he said.

"I haven't made up my mind to go," Dr. Morelle said.

"Hamburg's okay."

"I enjoy Paris. I always meet such interesting people."

"The people you want to meet," the other said, "are in Hamburg. Celeste is sure of it."

"I should be more impressed if she had taken the trouble to tell me all this herself."

De Goury nodded as if with understanding. "Fascinating girl," he said. "That's why she attracts attention wherever she goes, so much of it undesirable."

"Inspector Rommerque, for instance?"

"Precisely." The white-haired man spread out his hands. "You know how it is."

It was a dubious idea, yet somehow something about this man, and that remembered hint of an appeal in Celeste Ruz's eyes in the grubby little office at the Quai des Orfevres, seemed to insist that this was straight and level. She certainly had reason enough to decide that a meeting with him could result in her being dragged in by Inspector Rommerque's watch-dogs, and she might not want the information she had to give to be forced out of her by the detective. The information which was to send them both to Hamburg, for instance, on the Nord Express.

De Goury drained his glass. "You have seen one or two sides of a certain way of life, or living death, tonight. I would be pleased to complete your education before you leave Paris."

"I doubt if you can show me anything that I have not already witnessed," Dr. Morelle said cautiously.

The other drew a deep breath.

"I know everything about dope," he said with disarming frankness. "I have had everything; heroin, the needle, the pipe. I will not say it does you good, exactly, but if you go into a clinic now and then to get straightened out you escape the worst. I had a course just recently. Three weeks. At a splendid place. You would be interested to see the method of treatment. I became on good terms with the doctor running it. Would you like to pay it a visit?" He paused in his rush of words to smile slyly. "I mean, of course, merely to look it over."

It struck Dr. Morelle that this was another exhibitionist type, not so different from Inspector Rommerque, who was anxious to impress him with his close acquaintance with evil. While on the surface there appeared little to be learned that might prove of any value as a further lead, some intuition prompted him that he should go along with De Goury. At least he might let fall a revealing hint or two concerning Celeste Ruz.

"Where is it?"

"The Boulevard Bineau."

They took a taxi, the white-haired man still talking volubly all the way.

"A three weeks' disintoxication or 'straightening out' course is the minimum; not a cure, you understand, merely a cleansing of the system, undertaken for a fee of one hundred thousand francs. Mine cost me fifty thousand a week. I was expensive. Only twenty patients are received. They were getting the very best of everything, the softest 'let-down', the kindest way out from their respective kicks."

He stopped the taxi at the top of a quiet, tree-shadowed street, and they walked along to a large house set back in its own tree-enclosed grounds. The branches overhead sighed and rustled as they went up the semi-circular gravel drive. A wide door opened immediately to De Goury's ring, and as they went in he whispered to Dr. Morelle to walk gently, a warning which seemed scarcely necessary in view of the deep, silent carpet. The entrance-hall was wide and luxuriously furnished. The paintwork glistened white under the soft lighting.

De Goury led the way along a wide corridor off from the hall. He seemed to know his way about and the quiet-footed man who had opened the door had disappeared. Dr. Morelle caught the sound of groans issuing from one of the doors on his right.

"A woman just come in and hungry for her first re-lieving injection," the white-haired man explained, over his shoulder, as he listened outside the door. "Her husband is with her, take a peep."

In answer to his gentle tap-tap a white uniformed nurse opened the door and Dr. Morelle glimpsed the figure of a man beside a bed in the white room. He was holding the woman's hand who sighed and moaned and twisted in the bed. The restless head showed a very white face and brilliant eyes, black-encircled.

The door closed. "It would have been simple enough if she had just stuck to cocaine," De Goury said. "But like most of them, she takes morphine to quieten the cocaine-kick or to ease the nerve-torture. And this has led to dual addicition."

They went through a hall where half a dozen men and women were playing cards in silence while a nurse looked on.

"Here it is the gradual withdrawal idea," De Goury was saying. "Not the violent, sudden denial."

"Cold Turkey," Dr. Morelle said and his thoughts returned to that scented apartment on the Rue de Belle-chasse and the woman, Madame Babette. He remembered how scared she had been to talk to him, how that withdrawn look had taken possession of her, when he had begun to ask her questions. And now here was Celeste Ruz at first apparently anxious and willing to talk, sending this dope-addict in her place at the last minute.

As they continued through the house they heard hardly anyone speaking, neither patients, nurses nor doctors; whatever was said was in low tones. On the first floor where rested the patients commencing their treatment, Dr. Morelle glimpsed the flowers, pictures, glistening white walls and nickel fittings; each room had a bath attached, hot baths acting as nerve-calmers.

"When this room's occupant arrived a fortnight ago," De Goury said, outside a half-open door, "she was being perpetually suffocated by dozens of black cats, meowing and crowding in on her. She's now knitting downstairs. Been here twice before and sure enough she'll be seeing her cats again." A series of muffled shrieks pulled them up. The white-haired man nodded towards a room ahead. "Third day of deprivation. Her worst. It's only a nightmare she's having."

A little while later he and Dr. Morelle were leaving the house, as unobtrusively as they had entered it; returning the way they had come, along the quiet Boulevard Bineau, the trees whispering overhead, Dr. Morelle realized that the strange man by his side had still given no reason for having taken him to the house. He decided to put it down simply to the other's curious exhibition-istic streak.

It was only later after De Goury had seen him back to his hotel, chatting away as volubly as ever about his experiences in the drug-addict's underworld and he had reached his bedroom that Dr. Morelle realized that he had been neatly steered away from the vicinity of the bar where Celeste Ruz had arranged to meet him, and that the white-haired man had kept him in his sight continually. Had this been the other's motive? To keep him away from meeting the wild, drug-ridden girl chased from Carrin's villa by Inspector Rommerque's *flics*?

Why her message that she would meet him in Hamburg? Or was that another ruse of the white-haired man to get rid of him? In that case what was the link between the two? The girl must have confided in De Goury, otherwise he could not have brought her message to the bar.

Next morning Dr. Morelle spoke to Inspector Rommerque on the telephone and outlined the later events of last night. The detective's reaction was typically cryptic. "I will come and see you off on the Nord Express. That girl knew something; or the man who calls himself De Goury."

"You seem as anxious as they that I should go to Hamburg."

"If you choose not to make the trip, I shall certainly send someone," was the reply in Dr. Morelle's ear, "who will keep the rendezvous with Celeste Ruz in your place."

"Nevertheless," Dr. Morelle said, "I would like to

make sure that she has, in fact, left Paris for Hamburg herself."

Inspector Rommerque promptly supplied the address the girl had given in his office and suggested that he inquire there: Dr. Morelle hung up and went out of the hotel. But he might have saved himself the journey. Celeste Ruz had gone. He could learn nothing from the occupants of the house in a sleazy street off the Rue Muller leading down from Montmartre Hill, where she had her tawdry apartment; except that she had gone and no one knew when she would be back.

Preoccupied Dr. Morelle descended the worn steps of the Rue Muller and down the hill until he found a taxi, which took him back across the river to the Quai des Orfevres, and Inspector Rommerque's office. But the detective had not yet returned from some business which had called him out. Dr. Morelle left word that he was leaving for Hamburg that evening on the Nord Express and would Inspector Rommerque telephone him at his hotel.

The Nord Express was due out of the Gare du Nord at 19.57, arriving Hamburg 9.43 next morning. Dr. Morelle advised them at 60 Boulevard Gouvion St. Cyr of his plans, and reservations were made for him on the train and at the Vier Jahreszeiten, Hamburg. Interpol headquarters were alerted by the information with which he put them in the picture, especially the lead he had picked up pointing to Hamburg. There was already evidence that Western Germany was in the drug-traffic's grip; the rings had in the past routed the stuff down the Mediterranean, into Italy and through France, for ultimate disposal in the insatiable U.S.A. market. American garrisons in Western Germany had come to provide a new clientele; and the increasing activity of Hamburg's free port made it an ideal outlet for illicit narcotic-running to New York and neighbouring seaboards.

Before leaving his hotel Dr. Morelle had put a telephone-call through to Miss Frayle in London and let her know that he was leaving for Hamburg on the Nord Express that evening?"

"We are moving around, aren't we?" she said. "You'd better make the most of it, too; there's going to be so much work waiting for you when you do get back, you have no idea." He was impelled to remind her that he was not exactly engaged upon a holiday-spree, but decided to save it; it was just another of her typically thoughtless comments. Instead, he hinted at the luxurious style in which he was travelling, with everything laid on and all the police-forces of Europe giving him the full V.I.P. treatment. He hung up on her with the envious note in her voice echoing in his ear.

At the Gare du Nord he was surprised to find Inspector Rommerque, full of apologies for not having contacted him before, his explanation being that he had only recently got back to the Quai des Orfevres, by which time Dr. Morelle had left his hotel. They made their way along the platform together, the hiss of steam-engines, the animated voices of passengers and porters, and shrill whistles forcing Dr. Morelle to raise his tone as he gave a description of what had transpired last night, after he had left the detective. The other was frankly sceptical about Celeste Ruz's Hamburg idea, although he agreed with Interpol's estimate of the extent of the drug-running out of the port. "But I am convinced the top man operates from French soil," he said. "Most probably Paris."

They passed a newspaper-kiosk and Inspector Rommerque insisted on buying him the evening papers, a couple of magazines, Dr. Morelle declining a copy of *Le Vie Parisienne*, which the other kept for himself with an appropriate smirk. Dr. Morelle found his sleeping-compartment, where the porter had stowed his suit-cases. The detective stood on the platform for a final chat through the compartment-window, and waved him *bon voyage* as the train creaked and jarred, and then eased its way along the platform. Dr. Morelle ducked his head back into the compartment and closed the window.

He did not see Inspector Rommerque, still waving, but with his gaze intent upon each window slipping past, pause momentarily and give an imperceptible nod to a figure who stared back at him from a compartment as it moved along the platform.

Dr. Morelle had dropped the magazines and newspapers on his bed, and the jolt of the train starting had jerked the *Paris Soir* on to the floor. As he bent to pick it up, a headline glared up at him blackly. He read the story with eyes narrowed. It reported that the woman's body dragged out of the Seine early that morning had now been identified as Celeste Ruz. *Her tongue had been cut out.*

The Nord Express sped through the Paris suburbs while Dr. Morelle stood at the window without seeing the grimy façade of buildings broken by streets and alleys like spaces gaping between broken teeth in the dusk agleam with lights. He heard the compartment door open behind him, but remained motionless, without turning his head to answer the waiter come to take his order for dinner.

"*Bon soir*, Dr. Morelle."

It was a girl's voice, and Dr. Morelle swung round as if he had been struck.

It was Celeste Ruz.

Chapter Six

LEON STIERLIN was suave, dignified and carried a gold-headed walking stick, spoke English and French fluently, stayed only at the best hotels; and was on cordial terms with numerous dubious financiers and less reputable diplomats all over Europe.

Early in his Paris criminal career, the narcotics racket, Stierlin soon learned, was set up very much like any other business; manufacturers disposed of their product to large distributors, who in turn shipped the stuff to wholesalers in various parts of the world, the wholesalers dealt with local jobbers and the jobbers sold to the retailers, who dealt personally with the addicts.

Stierlin began as a distributor, purchasing drugs in lots of a hundred kilograms or more from European manufacturers, and sending them to wholesalers in the U.S.A. He never had the slightest contact with addicts, seldom even saw the drugs themselves.

He was simply a respectable business man who negotiated with factory sales-managers, made arrangements with forwarding companies, exchanged telegrams in cipher with his agents in Europe and cables with America, made deposits and withdrawals at various banks, and generally attended to work that was performed on typewriters, telephones and calculating-machines. Many of his retailers were addicts, he knew.

"But no one who holds a position of any importance

in the racket is so stupid as to use drugs himself," he would tell his associates, whenever he did take anyone so much into his confidence.

On a trip to New York Stierlin had met a broad-shouldered Turk, named Kalyick, a so-called tobacco-importer, who was cleaning up importing drugs. After huddles with Kalyick for several days and meeting with a number of other interested characters, Stierlin set himself up in an apartment which lay in the Eiffel Tower's shadow when the midday sun shone; realizing that the key to power in the drug-traffic was the control of sources of supply, he focused his attention on two drug-companies he knew, one near Arras, and the other in Brittany.

Stierlin's technique for securing the control of the product of the two factories was simplicity itself. He demanded more drugs from them than they could conveniently supply, and then offered them such attractive prices, they gladly accepted his financial backing in order to expand. He was able to pull this operation off because of Kalyick's enormous requirements for the U.S. market.

The two factories' major problem of supply lay in their inability to pay for the huge amounts of raw opium they needed to manufacture the drugs; it required one pound of opium to make about two ounces of morphine. What Stierlin did was to advance both firms enough cash to buy the opium, in return for an option on every gramme of the as yet unmanufactured drugs.

He virtually bossed the narcotics racket in France.

In Paris one of Stierlin's acquaintances was an ex-diplomat who supplied diplomatic couriers to anyone who wanted contraband smuggled across the border without being detected by customs inspectors. Soon Stierlin was using almost every port in Europe to ship his merchandise out; he had representatives in Istanbul, Athens, Constanza, Trieste, Alexandria; he had fat bank-accounts in London, Paris and New York and several other American cities.

Stierlin made several trans-Atlantic trips to personally deliver goods to Kalyick. One day he arrived in New York with 150 kilograms for Kalyick and checked into a midtown hotel where the other joined him. He gave Kalyick 50 kilos only, saying he would keep the other 100 until the other paid up. A few hours later Kalyick returned, bleeding copiously, and reported that the drugs had been hijacked from his car.

Stierlin was pondering what to do next when a New York hood named Ruby walked in. Ruby said he had heard there had been some trouble, could he be of any assistance?

Stierlin told him about the hijacking. "See what I can fix," Ruby said, and left. He returned later with 30 kilos of the missing drugs, which wasn't so tricky since he had arranged the hijacking in the first place, and said that was all he could recover.

Stierlin wasn't upset about the other 20 kilos; Ruby was obviously entitled to them as a commission for returning the thirty. Ruby suggested moving the remaining drugs to another hotel. "They can be under my protection."

For this idea Stierlin cared hardly at all, but he was alone in New York and so the move was made, and a Ruby mobster was assigned to guard the drugs.

Next morning he was found with his wrists slashed

and the drugs gone. Stierlin couldn't be sure whether Ruby had stolen the drugs himself, whether Kalyick had stolen them from Ruby, or whether it was some entirely different mob. So it was not all plain sailing for Stierlin.

"I wrote the trip off as experience," he was to say later.

American importers, when they got his drugs into the U.S., adulterated them by fifty per cent, selling an adulterated kilogram to a wholesaler for something like 500 dollars. The wholesaler adulterated the drugs some more; so did the retailer. By the time the drugs reached the addicts, who bought by the ounce or fraction of an ounce, a pure, unadulterated Stierlin kilogram represented two or three thousand dollars gross income.

Stierlin dropped Kalyick in favour of a New York drug-trafficker named Nathan, a stout moist man with considerable experience from his Lower East Side youth. After a trip to Paris to confer with Stierlin, Nathan returned to New York, accompanied by two trunks. In the false bottom of each was 25 kilograms of morphine.

From Paris Stierlin continued to send double-bottomed trunks, which would be put aboard ship in the name of some passenger. When the trunks were safely aboard, Nathan would be notified by a cable signed with the name under which the trick trunks were being shipped. Nathan would meet the ship, locate the trunks on the dock, affix forged customs inspection stamps on them while no one was looking, and have the trunks carted past the barrier. He was entrusted with disposing of the drugs in New York.

Stierlin's trunks never contained less than 25 kilograms of drugs each, and the scheme for getting the trunks past the U.S. Customs proved very successful; Nathan had a pal in the shape of a customs inspector who felt the service's pay-scale was much too low.

The New York end of the business becoming more complex than the Paris end, which was strictly routine, Nathan took another trafficker, named Berg, into partnership. Five successful shipments later, Nathan informed Berg of Stierlin's identity. He also told Stierlin about his new partner.

Stierlin was anxious to meet Berg personally. Nathan was happy about his arrangements just as they were. He didn't want Berg to meet anyone. Stierlin insisted, however, and a Paris meeting between the three of them was fixed.

Stierlin proved charming and hospitable, but what he wanted was precisely what Nathan didn't want him to have. "Fifty per cent of the American profits, now the New York end's doing so well." Stierlin had once been happy with the price he got for the drugs, which anyway gave him twenty-five per cent clear profit. The trio agreed to meet the following day. Stierlin took Berg on a tour of his warehouse. Nathan wasn't invited.

At the warehouse, which contained several hundred kilos of drugs, Stierlin entertained Berg lavishly, promised to provide him with all the stuff he wanted, and urged him to cut out Nathan.

Berg finally agreed to let Stierlin deliver him a shipment of 100 kilos of heroin, 75 of which was purchased by Berg and 25 of which he was to sell for Stierlin. Nathan was told nothing about it.

Arriving in New York, Berg sat by his telephone for a week. He was waiting for news of his trunks. One night he got a call from a mysterious man who refused to identify himself. "You are to take a cab to Ninth Avenue and Forty-Seventh Street. You will find another cab parked. You get in the other cab."

Berg followed instructions and found inside the second cab a short dark man who silently held out a torn half of a business card which Berg had given Stierlin in Paris. Berg pulled the other half out of his pocket; the two pieces fitted together. The short dark man said the trunks from Stierlin were waiting for Berg at a down-town hotel.

Berg went alone in the taxi to the hotel, in a dark side-street, and a man came out of the hotel, got into the taxi, quietly stabbed Berg in the heart, cut out his tongue and pushed him out of the taxi, which drove off again—to Nathan's headquarters.

Stierlin had tipped off Nathan that Berg was double-crossing him. Nathan was not only grateful for the tip-off, he also began to get the idea. He went to Paris and agreed with Stierlin that after mature consideration, he had reached the conclusion that Stierlin should receive a fifty per cent cut of the American profits.

Stierlin smiled and clasped Nathan's hand.

Stierlin had long since cultivated the acquaintance of Inspector Rommerque of the Sûreté, reaching an understanding with him of considerable mutual advantage. Rommerque agreed to give Stierlin a clear field, in return for 250,000 francs a month; Rommerque was to take care of any rival traffickers. "This will help you," he told Stierlin, "to keep out competition, while I can build up an impressive record, allay suspicion regarding myself."

On his trip to Paris for his business-chat with Stierlin, Nathan on the boat had picked up a leggy, bosomy blonde New York ex-showgirl, Winsome Deans. Stierlin went for her in a big way, which did not pass unnoticed by Nathan. He decided that the moment for a show-down with his partner had arrived and two days after the handshake he confronted Stierlin with the bland announcement that from now on he was taking over. That Stierlin was charmed by this unexpected about-face was not strictly true. However, Nathan had re-vealed that he had 50,000 dollars at his disposal with which he proposed to buy out the other, so Stierlin con-cealed his reaction and pretended to agree to Nathan as boss.

Stierlin agreed to sell Nathan all the morphine then in his possession as part of the 50,000 dollars take-over deal, and to see that it was shipped to the U.S. It would be advisable, he counselled, to divide the merchandise into two parts, so that not so much would be lost in the event of seizure by the American Customs.

The first shipment was to be sent in three trunks, each of which would contain packages of morphine in cubes. When he had completed all the preliminary prepara-tions, Stierlin allowed Nathan to inspect the shipment, and told him that it would arrive in New York in July and that he had better hurry back to get it. Somewhat trustfully leaving Winsome Deans in Paris, Nathan sailed for Quebec on the Empress of Scotland. In due course he received a cable from Paris: "Sister arriving *Innoku*, Black Diamond Line Hoboken, July 18th."

Meanwhile in Paris, Stierlin had Nathan's 50,000 dollars, and Winsome Deans. As soon as the *Innoku* had left Antwerp, he tipped off Inspector Rommerque about the shipment, who in turn tipped off the American authorities. The ship got to Hoboken and was promptly overrun by customs men, who had little difficulty in locating the drugs. A hundred and fifty dollars a kilogram reward for information leading to narcotics seizures was the New York Narcotics Bureau's price, so Rommerque came into enough dollars to make him feel exceptionally well-disposed towards Stierlin.

A few days later a body was found in an abandoned car in a down-town New York alley, its tongue was missing. The dead man was Nathan.

Stierlin now decided to shift his headquarters. His first idea was to get out of Europe entirely, the going was getting too hot for his comfort, but America was, after all, his best market and Western Europe his best jumping-off board, only the best was good enough for Stierlin.

He set up receiving and transmitting stations all over Europe, and chose Hamburg as his base, because Germany was full of good alkaloid chemists and manufacturing facilities; and Hamburg was a free port, and commerce in free ports was virtually unrestricted.

Some time before it was known that Stierlin was shifting his headquarters to Hamburg, the New York Narcotics Bureau planted an undercover agent in Paris. She was a big-boned brunette from Marseilles.

Her name was Celeste Ruz.

Chapter Seven

THE NORD EXPRESS sped on into the black, starless night.

In the luxurious restaurant-car, the white table-cloth gleamed, the cutlery and wine-glasses glinted under the soft light; waiters moved past expertly and the aroma of cigars lay on the air-conditioned atmosphere; and Dr. Morelle watched Celeste Ruz over his coffee-cup. Celeste Ruz had reached the end of her story which she had begun an hour or so before in his sleeping-compartment. She made a distinct contrast to the dope-addict, the role she had played in Inspector Rommerque's office.

She wore a figure-clinging dress; draped around her shoulders was a dark-grey stole, over which spilled her black hair. Her dark eyes were clear, animated, and the taut expression she wore when she had made her dramatic, totally unexpected appearance had relaxed. It was almost as if, he thought, that recounting her strange adventures and the knowledge which she had absorbed as a result had released the pent-up tension inside her. The mental strain of carrying such highly inflammable material was enough to give the nerves of the toughest police-agent ragged edges, even to snapping point.

Dr. Morelle wondered how long Inspector Rommerque would remain fooled by the newspaper reports of her death, which she had, aided by New York Narcotics Bureau operators, so neatly engineered. He leaned forward and opened his thin gold cigarette case. She took a Le Sphinx, and her fingers still trembled slightly, he noticed. The tension had not entirely receded from her nerves and muscles. The shadow of the fearsome figure, Leon Stierlin still reached out to her with all its dark menace.

"The bureau had many facts already," she was saying. "Only they didn't know who the big wheel was." Dr. Morelle found himself unable to resist the reflection that if the forces of law and order were corrupted by individuals like Inspector Rommerque, it was remarkable that such a big advance had been achieved towards clearing up the drug-trafficking. Who was to be trusted? This young woman opposite him now, how was he to be certain that she was not playing some twisted game of double-bluff? "The facts of his large-scale operations were known; it was his name that had to be filled in. I did that only a week ago. I discovered it," the girl continued, "while I was working as a member of Carrin's mob."

"It was then that you learned Stierlin had shifted his headquarters to Hamburg?"

"Carrin had come to feel he was being treated badly. In the mood he was in he grew careless, and it was easy for me to find out who and where the boss was."

"It explains why Stierlin instructed Rommerque to pick him up." Dr. Morelle took a drag at his cigarette, and Celeste Ruz nodded. "It also explains why Rommerque chose that particular time for the raid, if he had long been aware of Carrin's activities."

"It was a double-punch idea; it would oblige Stierlin,

and impress you." She tapped the ash of her cigarette. "Anyway the noose was already drawing closer round that damned *flic*'s neck. The tip-offs that New York had. It began to look fishy. How was it, the bureau started to ask, that the stuff was never detained before it left Europe?"

Dr. Morelle said through a puff of cigarette-smoke. "I was wondering how long it would take someone to realize that whenever the drugs failed the reach the purchaser, whoever was marketing them had nevertheless been paid in advance."

"Exactly," Celeste Ruz said. "Therefore Rommerque was being tipped off by someone in Europe—Paris—who knew what they were talking about all right. Someone in there close to the top man."

This was why, because suspicion had fallen on the man at the Quai des Orfrevres, that Interpol, who had a line with the New York Bureau, had instructed the girl to contact Dr. Morelle with the utmost discretion. "I had a hunch that the *flic* was suspicious of me." She shrugged. "I don't know how or why he should have found out."

"De Goury, you sent in your place?"

"Just an addict who has been useful to me. He thinks I am on the kick. I phoned, and then was forced to postpone our meeting until now; his job was to prevent you from becoming too curious, and trying to find me."

"An engaging personality," Dr. Morelle said. "What happens if he should inform Inspector Rommerque of what he knows concerning you and me?"

"I don't think Rommerque would be able to do much

about it. His days are numbered already." She sounded supremely confident. She went on to enlarge upon her line of operation in Hamburg.

"Stierlin is somewhere around, that is all we know. I have to contact an agent when I arrive." This agent knew the route the top man was using to get his opium out of his Middle East supply centres. "By sea to Venice; there it's repacked and shipped by rail through the Brenner Pass to Innsbruck, where it's stored until it's taken to Hamburg."

The speed of the express seemed to have slackened. Dr. Morelle stared out of the window, seeing only his own reflection and that of Celeste Ruz and the shaded lights of their table against the darkness outside. His mind wrapped itself round the risks and dangers that lay ahead for the next few days. It was necessary that he and the extraordinary young woman opposite him could work out a *modus operandi*. The situation looked as if it was going to be hazardous; Hamburg was unlikely to prove a rest-cure for either of them, and he wanted to know where they were going.

Celeste Ruz appeared to share his speculations, she, too, lapsed into silence; then there was a movement beside him and a figure bowed to the girl. Dr. Morelle glanced round as the waiter said hesitantly: *"Pardon s'il vous plait."*

Celeste Ruz looked up at him inquiringly.

"There is a little difficulty about your sleeping-compartment. Another passenger is confusing it with his. If you would be so kind and explain to this other passenger, who will not be satisfied by what we tell him, you understand?"

The girl frowned at him. "I am sure I am in the right compartment."

"Of course, of course. It is just that this other passenger insists that he has been given it."

Celeste Ruz muttered impatiently and then with a smile at Dr. Morelle got up and followed by the other man, full of protestations of apology, went out of the restaurant-car. Dr. Morelle glimpsed the way in which her dress revealed the curves of her tall, well-built figure, caught the wave of expensive scent that remained after her, and reflected again upon the toughness and resourceful character beneath her feminine exterior.

He scowled to himself suddenly, and took long, thoughtful drags at his cigarette. He felt disturbed, and the uneasy feeling grew as the Le Sphinx shortened in his fingers. Then he realized what it was. It was the man the girl had accompanied back to her compartment. How had he known who she was? He had not mentioned her name when he spoke to her. Obviously he had been positive of her identity. Dr. Morelle glanced round. There were plenty of other people in the restaurant-car; several women, any of whom might have been occupying the compartment to which the man had referred. But he had picked out Celeste Ruz unerringly.

Dr. Morelle got to his feet. He went swiftly in the direction taken by Celeste Ruz and the man. The train's speed seemed to have picked up once more, it was moving fast, clattering and rolling across points; and amidst the noise came the eerie screech of its whistle.

He recalled the girl had mentioned to him that her sleeping-compartment was located three doors beyond his, in the same coach. The swaying, brightly-lit corridor was deserted, only his gaunt figure was reflected in the windows as he made his way quickly and noiselessly past the closed compartment-doors.

He gained his own compartment and went on until he stood outside Celeste Ruz's door. There was no sign of the man who had come to the restaurant-car in search of her. He rapped on the door. There was no reply. He rapped again, more loudly. Still no reply. He turned the door-handle, half-expecting it to be locked. The door opened and he stepped into darkness. He snapped on the light-switch. The compartment was empty. It was hers all right; her scent filled his nostrils.

A thought occurred to him and he went out, closing her door after him. Swift strides took him back along the corridor. It was still deserted, though he fancied he heard the noise of a compartment-door slamming shut further along the train. He paused a moment to see if anyone should put in an appearance. It might be the girl. But nobody came from the direction of the sound. It may not have been anyone; it may have been a slap of rushing air against the speeding express. He turned the handle of his own compartment door and threw it open.

He stood frozen on the threshold for an instant and then plunged into the compartment.

Celeste Ruz was hanging from a coat-hanger hook by one of his silk neckties notted round her throat, and her feet placed at the other end of his bed, so that the weight of her body suspended across the compartment was choking the life out of her. As the figure swayed grotesquely before him, he moved forward. He lifted her up bodily so that her weight no longer dragged her down, while he quickly undid the tie round her neck. It

had bitten into her white flesh and her face was con-
torted as he laid her on the bed, while he bent over her.

Her eyes were closed, but as his fingers found her pulse
he felt a faint spark of life.

He straightened Celeste Ruz flat on the bed, face upwards, while pushing the pillows under the small of her
back so that her shoulders inclined downwards but did
not touch the bed. With unhurried speed he bent her
head and neck as far back as possible, and raised her
hands above her head. He knelt over her hips, and his
steely hands began their work, the thumb-tips together,
the ball of each thumb just beneath the margin of the
girl's ribs, the fingers each in the space between two ribs.
Now he was pressing her ribs upwards and inwards with
his hands. His face almost touched her as he strove to
press the air out of her lungs.

He gave a final sharp push, at the same time taking
his hands away, and knelt upright for a moment, so as to
let her lungs expand. He continued the same action a
dozen times.

Suddenly she took a long, shuddering breath and she
opened her eyes, stared at him vacantly for a few
moments before recognition flashed across her face and
she contrived a wan smile. "I should have been more
careful," she said in a painfully husky whisper.

"I fear I must hold myself to blame," he said.

Her fingers closed over his as she gave a slight shake
of her head. Her eyes flickered shut again; and then
she opened them and forced herself to sit up. She looked
around her and then managed another rasping whisper.

"I don't think I should be here. What would people
say?"

He was pouring her out a glass of water from a carafe. He came back to her and held the glass to her mouth. "Doubtless that was the idea," he said. "Not very original, but it would have required some explaining, a beautiful young woman hanged in my sleeping-compartment with my tie."

She repressed a shudder and her hand crept to her neck, where the livid weal spread obliquely towards each ear. He was telling her what had made him suspicious of the man who had tricked her almost to her death.

"Suddenly, as we were passing your door," she said huskily, "he opened it—I was ahead of him—and he dragged me inside, knocking me half-unconscious." Dr. Morelle had noted the bruise on the side of her jaw.

"It is a warning of danger from a quarter other than Stierlin's," he said.

She regarded him with slight puzzlement. "But this was one of Stierlin's agents," she said.

She choked painfully and he gave her a shake of the head. He held the glass of water for her to sip from, which she took from him and drank gratefully. "Had that been the case," he murmured, "you would have found speaking even more difficult—minus a tongue."

The rim of the glass rattled against her teeth. A terrible shiver ran through her entire body. She closed her eyes, screwing them up tightly as if to shut out the mental picture his words had conjured up. Then her dark gaze fastened upon him again.

"Who was it?" She mouthed the query over the glass which she was gripping hard.

"Inspector Rommerque would be a good bet."

"That dirty *flic*," she rasped contemptuously. He

shrugged and she smoothed a hand down her ruffled skirt and then swung her slender legs off the bed, her expensively stockinged toes curling for the high-heeled shoes which she had lost during the attack on her. There was a glint in her gaze as she let it wander round the compartment, taking in the travel-stained and garish-labelled suitcases, the silver, monogrammed hairbrushes on the narrow shelf, the tooth-brushes and toothpaste neatly placed above the wash-bowl.

It crossed Dr. Morelle's mind that this extraordinary young woman, tough and completely without fear, was recovering very quickly from the effects of the savage attempt on her life.

He was about to add further to his speculation concerning the Quai des Orfevres detective, instead he stood tensed for a fraction of a second, and then moved to the door and wrenched it open. She saw the back of his dark head, his broad shoulders tapering down to lean hips framed in the doorway, as he glanced up and down the corridor. Then he turned back into the compartment.

"I fancied I heard someone," he said, closing the door; and with a long drawn-out screech the Nord Express tore into a tunnel and the noise was deafening as it ate into the pitch blackness.

Chapter Eight

Miss Frayle came up the steps of the tube-station at Oxford Circus, and paused, hatless and fair-haired, to adjust her horn-rimmed glasses on her tip-tilted nose. Her large eyes behind the lenses blinked up at the slice of sky between the tall buildings. The late spring sun had been shining when she had hurried down to the tube earlier that morning; now the sky was a bluish-grey, and a chill draught moulded her dress round her slim figure.

She would walk the short distance to Harley Street, and set off briskly across Oxford Street, pausing only a few moments to window-shop at the corner fashion-store, before continuing in the direction of Broadcasting House.

She had been cooped up in the solicitor's Blooms-bury office most of the morning, and now it was twelve-forty-five. Mr. Throwton smoked a pipe, and kept his windows closed so that his small office had become stuffy, and he had taken an interminable time producing the deeds, leather-bound books and other documents which concerned this client of his in Cornwall who was so anxious for Dr. Morelle to handle an investigation of supernatural ramifications concerning a vanished family heirloom and an old will.

It was a matter in which Dr. Morelle hadn't the slightest interest, but he had been unable to discourage

Throwton or his client; and as a result of Dr. Morelle's
absorption with his trip abroad, Miss Frayle herself had
forgotten all about it. Some of the documents had been
sent up from Cornwall to Dr. Morelle direct, and though
they had been returned promptly to the solicitor's office,
he had apparently mislaid them. Eventually Miss Frayle
decided that the only way of convincing Mr. Throwton
that he had the papers in his possession was to go through
the files with him at his office. She had accordingly
gone along to Bloomsbury at ten-thirty that morning;
and after a lot of searching the documents had turned
up. But not before Miss Frayle had endured long dis-
cussions between the solicitor and his partner, an even
older and vaguer individual than Mr. Throwton; she
had awaited while files had been found and consulted;
and at the end of it all, both men had insisted that they
would delay advising their client to engage someone else
to take on the case until Dr. Morelle returned. They still
believed that he could be persuaded to change his mind
and interest himself in this Cornish mystery.

Miss Frayle felt irritated at her complete failure to
convince them that Dr. Morelle's mind was implacably
made up; she knew he would blame her when they
started worrying him again when he came back to London.

She put the thought of Mr. Throwton's and his blessed
client's obstinacy out of her mind, and began to wonder
how Dr. Morelle had enjoyed his stay in Paris. Although
she knew it quite well she still entertained the sneaking
suspicion that it was a city of sin, and that Dr. Morelle
would become involved in some wicked, unimaginable
orgy. Still, he was in Hamburg by now, and well out of

the way of temptation *à la Parisienne*. She smiled to herself at the ridiculous way her mind ran on; and felt thankful that the hurrying passers-by could not read her thoughts.

It was at that moment that she caught sight of the headline on the midday edition of an evening paper. The newspaper-seller stood opposite the towering building that was Broadcasting House and as she passed him and he turned away from his box in which the papers were stacked, to serve a customer, she read: *Train Accident In Germany.*

She told herself it couldn't be, of course. But when she at last could quiet the racing of her heart enough to buy a newspaper, she found it was the Nord Express. The train on which Dr. Morelle had told her he was travelling when he had telephoned from Paris the previous evening.

Her eyes wide she scanned the brief report beneath the black headlines. The train had been de-railed outside Bremen. The full story had not yet been received. No passengers were named; but casualties were expected to be light.

Miss Frayle, unconscious of the people milling past her, tried to extract some comfort from the last part of the report. But she could not stem the great wave of anxiety that swept over her. Dr. Morelle was on the train and something dreadful must have happened to him, that was what filled her mind. She tried desperately to pull herself together, to steel herself against the shock.

Her weakness lasted no more than a few seconds; her will-power flowed back as she told herself she must get to

Harley Street without delay, and clutching the news-paper, she hurried on.

It seemed to take ages before she reached 221b Harley Street; she half-ran, half-walked, and as she let herself in she was distraught and breathless; but she knew who she was going to turn to for advice. Inspector Hood of Scotland Yard.

As she stood in the hall, she suddenly remembered the B.B.C. news bulletin. She dashed to the study and switched on the radio. The calm, detached voice of the news-reader came on the air, but she realized he was already half-way through his newscast, and he wound up without any reference to the train-accident in Germany. The news-reader's voice droned on with the weather reports, and Miss Frayle switched it off impatiently. She was not interested in the weather. She had to get news of Dr. Morelle.

She picked up the telephone.

Just at the moment when he was told he was wanted on the phone by Miss Frayle, Inspector Hood happened to be thinking of Dr. Morelle. He was down in the musty basement of the turreted old building overlooking the Embankment, where a couple of rooms were taken up by the Black Museum, with its shelf upon shelf of curious and repellent exhibits. Inspector Hood had been chewing his worn pipe and eyeing the frieze, just below the ceiling, of death-masks of British criminals of bygone days. They had been collected at a time when forensic theorists like Lombroso believed that a face made up of the dominant characteristics of various criminals' features, would provide a typical picture of the criminal. And Inspector Hood had recalled listening to Dr.

Morelle lecturing on the subject: how, in 1913, after several years' study, a committee reported that measurements and physical anomalies in criminals presented a startling conformity with similar statistics of law-abiding citizens, with the inevitable conclusion that there was no such thing as a physical criminal type.

The Lombroso death-masks had found a home in the sinister-named Black Museum; that of Heinrich Himmler, German Gestapo Chief, taken a few hours after he chewed a cyanide-phial when overtaken by his British captors, was now included among them; there were numerous other murder-exhibits with which Inspector Hood was familiar. A human finger preserved in alcohol, a bloodstained matchstick, a piece of carbon-paper, a twisted can-opener, a small piece of bone once part of a human voice-box, which had helped him bring a murderer to justice.

He was recalling that it was Dr. Morelle who had grasped the significance of that fragment which could be snapped by the pressure of two fingers, when the sergeant in charge of the Black Museum came and interrupted his thoughts. He didn't tell Miss Frayle it was Dr. Morelle who had been in his thoughts.

"I was just thinking of you, Miss Frayle," he said. "It just shows, doesn't it?"

"It's this train crash in Germany," Miss Frayle said breathlessly. "Have you heard about it? The Nord Express. It's in the papers. Dr. Morelle was on it. He telephoned last night from Paris that he was catching the Nord Express to Hamburg. I'm so worried, Inspector Hood."

"I knew he was in Paris," Inspector Hood said, and

now his voice sounded a little anxious. "But I hadn't heard he'd left for Hamburg."

"It was some sudden idea. He must have found some important lead to send him dashing off there."

"I can check up on all this," Inspector Hood said. "I mean, if he changed his mind to go at the last minute, he might have changed his mind again and not gone."

"He would have phoned me if he'd done that."

"I see."

"I ought to go to Hamburg," Miss Frayle said. "He may need me."

"Don't do anything for the next half-hour," Inspector Hood said reassuringly. "I'll get on to Interpol; they're sure to know. I'll phone you back as soon as I can."

Miss Frayle thanked him and hung up. It was her lunch-time and although she had no appetite, to take her mind away from all the unpleasant possibilities that the news of the disaster had conjured up, she made herself an omelette and some coffee. She toyed with the omelette on a tray in the study and was drinking her third cup of coffee. She nearly sent the tray flying as she grabbed the telephone when it rang.

"Afraid there's no news," Inspector Hood told her. "Paris say that he was certainly on the Nord Express, so far as they know. They're in touch with the German police and we'll know what's happened as soon as they know."

Miss Frayle was silent for a moment. "I'll have to get to Hamburg myself, as soon as I can," she said.

"If you really think you should."

"I'll find him all right," Miss Frayle went on. "Even if he isn't hurt, he may have suffered a shock. I'm sure he'll be glad of someone to be with him. Is there a plane for Hamburg this afternoon?"

"Leave all that to me," he said. "I'll lay the whole thing on. If you feel you ought to go, we'll see you get there, quick."

"Oh, thank you," Miss Frayle said.

"See your passport's in order and begin packing. I'll phone you back and give you the drill."

She checked her passport, and then she went through her clothes for the weekend case she always kept ready for just such an emergency ever since she had worked for Dr. Morelle.

Now, the minutes passed in a flurry of excitement and activity.

Just before three o'clock Inspector Hood was back on the telephone again. She was booked on the Lufthansa plane leaving London Airport five-five. A detective from the Hamburg police department would meet her at Hamburg airport. Inspector Hood made a joke of it, saying he hoped she was packed; he would see to it that a police-car would call for her to take her to London Airport. She could not help feeling thrilled and important. She thanked him over and over.

"You won't have a motor-cycle escort as well," he chuckled, "like you would in a Hollywood film, but you'll do all right."

It was only after she had hung up that she realized he had not received any further news of Dr. Morelle.

When sometime later the door-bell rang Miss Frayle hurried into the hall with her suitcase. She had coped with advising everyone who ought to know what had happened, racking her brains in an effort to recall if there was a thing she had missed taking care of. Had she forgotten anything terribly important? The police-car driver took her case and she started to follow him.

As she turned to close the door she heard the tele-phone shrill. She rushed back to the study, her heart banging wildly, praying it was Dr. Morelle. She scooped up the receiver.

It was a wrong number.

Chapter Nine

Iᴛ ᴡᴀs round about the time when Miss Frayle in London was reading the newspaper report of the Nord Express disaster.

The man stood in front of a bookstall at the top of the steps on Hamburg-Hauptbahnof, staring absently at the newspapers, glossy magazines and the colourful display of books. His mind was unable to register anything of what he saw. For several minutes he had been growing aware of a mounting sense of strangeness and confusion. Now, with an almost jarring suddenness, he realized why.

He was lost. Lost and nameless in the depths of Hamburg's main railway-station. His first reaction was one of panic. He moved away jerkily from the steps which led down to the long, busy platforms beneath the glass roof, through which the blue sky showed where the smoke-grimed patches were clearer. He continued past the bookstall and found himself at an exit, out of which spilled the busy throng on to the Glockengiesserwall, where the trams clanged past.

He stood there for a moment irresolutely, unable to recall the few moments which it had taken him to walk from the bookstall to this point. He was on his own among a crowd of strangers He appeared to stand aside, to be watching the hustle and movement, hearing the voices and traffic-noise from the outside.

A coloured sign overhead caught his eye. He stared

at it uncomprehendingly, and then the next thing he remembered he was walking. He thought that he had never felt so hot. His shirt was soaking wet, his joints were stiff, his feet ached. Maybe he'd been running?

He was in some street and had a vague feeling that he was trying to get away from something. Or perhaps he had got away? He was tired, and had a sudden, urgent desire to take a bath and a rest. He walked on, at a more leisurely pace.

The street he found himself in was narrow, the buildings overcrowded. The houses were small and grimy, and behind them the black roofs of warehouses sloped up, and in the distance the steel, pointing finger of a crane. The tangy smell of the sea was in his nostrils; there came the low, mournful note of a ship's siren. He was in the dock area. He didn't know where the street would take him. He didn't much care so long as it continued.

Presently, the façade changed, they were still old houses, but larger. There were two or three shops, and a beer-cellar, and eventually an hotel. It was small, the brickwork drab, but the windows and wide entrance door had been freshly painted in some shade of dark green.

He paused outside, then went up the two steps and into a small square hall. There was a reception-desk at the side of the narrow stairs with an alcove behind it. There were shelves at the back of the alcove with some tattered books lying on them, and a board dotted with hooks and keys at one side of the shelves.

He pressed the bell on the desk, and a plump woman in a grey dress appeared.

The man had no luggage and there was nothing in his notecase except mark notes in tens and twenties. As he opened the case the woman's eyes fastened on the notes, he had a faint recollection of obtaining the notes at the railway-station. Had he exchanged some other currency for them? The recollection vanished.

"Have you a room?"

"First-floor back."

She took the money he held out to her, and then led him upstairs, along a narrow landing where the paper was peeling off the walls. She opened a door and stood aside inviting him to enter. He went in and the woman muttered something which he didn't catch, and she went out and closed the door.

He glanced dubiously around; the paper on the walls, faded and stained, in one place there was a splash-mark which looked as if a bottle of wine had been smashed against the wall.

No wardrobe; just a corner curtained off with hooks for hanging clothes. There was a chest-of-drawers with the beading chipped and there were grease-stains on the top. There was no wash-basin and the window-curtains were of the same faded material as the bedspread. When he pulled this back he saw that the bedclothes were grubby and looked as though they hadn't been changed in months.

In disgust he turned away and peered out of the window. He overlooked a yard and a shed. Beyond was another brick building with other sheds adjoining. The doors of the building gaped open and he could see a man hosing the concrete floor; but the dark stains on the concrete were still visible. He realized the place was a slaughter-house.

The bed creaked and sagged as he sat on it, as if

about to fall apart. He stared at his dusty shoes and beyond them to the ragged scrap of carpet covering the
centre of the linoleum. He kept telling himself it was no
good; he'd have to get out. A sudden burst of laughter
seeped through the wall from the next room. A woman's
laughter; and then he heard the murmuring of voices.

He got up and opened the door, then hesitated as the
door of the neighbouring room was thrown open and a
girl and a man came out. The girl was young and her
face might have been pretty if it hadn't been buried beneath the make-up. Her hair was blonde. She wore a
tight thin blouse through which the outline of her bra
was revealed and a short skirt slit up either side. Each
step she took revealed her legs above the knee. The man
pushed his hat on the back of his head and put his arm
around the girl's waist. She closed the door and the pair
went downstairs.

He waited and then he went out of his room and down
to the hall. It was deserted. The woman appeared and
stared at him questioningly.

"I won't be needing the room," he said. She shrugged
and turned away. "What about my money?"

"If you don't want to stay, that's up to you. Not my
fault you've changed your mind. I'm not going to be the
loser."

She was gone and there was no one for him to argue
with. He was too tired to argue, anyway. He was thankful to get outside into the cleaner air of the street.

He suddenly realized he was walking quickly. He
slowed up, glancing about him, looking for somewhere
with a suitable room. He had to be more careful. He
continued along the street, then turned into a wide

thoroughfare. It looked more prosperous, the shops were larger, although he still appeared to be near the docks. There was still the sense of the sea not far distant.

He found a hotel at the end of the block, and went in. It looked clean. It was far from luxurious, but it appeared comfortable. The man at the reception desk said there was a room vacant. The room was on the third floor. It was pleasant enough with a wash-basin and a full-sized wardrobe. He closed the door. The bed-clothes were all right and there was a dressing-table with an oval mirror. He had no comb or brushes; only the things he stood up in. He gazed at his reflection in the mirror.

He decided from the look of his chin-stubble that he had not shaved that morning. His dark suit was crumpled, and his shirt and collar creased and grubby. But he wasn't much interested. He turned away and flopped down on the bed and went to sleep.

It was a little past two by his wrist-watch when he awakened streaming with sweat, but he felt refreshed. The afternoon sun streamed in, he hadn't drawn the curtains shut. Almost at once a wave of restlessness swept over him. He swung himself off the bed and went down the stairs to the street.

He had to get going. It didn't matter where. To keep going, that was it. So long as he was out. That was all he wanted. He felt hemmed in. Otherwise he felt all right. And as soon as he started walking he was fine. He completely relaxed. He wasn't going anywhere and there wasn't any hurry.

He walked along, looking in the shop-windows with a casual interest. He found himself standing outside a barber's shop, his fingers were grazing the stubble on his chin. Impulsively, he went in; there was a vacant chair and he went straight to it. The barber hovered round him, chatting away.

He felt fresher, but glad to be out on the street again. It had begun to feel stuffy in the shop, and he'd got restless once more. He couldn't have sat still any longer. But it was pleasant now, just walking along and watching the people and enjoying the sights of the market he had come to. Fruit-stalls and women selling clothing and stockings. Stalls with wonderful food, cheeses, cakes, long black sausage, big yellow tomatoes.

He stopped at one stall and bought a couple of apples. Somehow everything seemed new and different to him, picturesque. Even the people. But he couldn't become absorbed in it; he had to leave them, as if he was right outside the teeming world about him, he had to keep going.

He stood outside a bookshop-window full of books and pictures. Gazing in at the pictures he suddenly felt the apples in his pocket. He stood there until he had eaten them both.

He didn't remember if he'd had any lunch. He felt very warm and violently thirsty. But he kept going, now searching for somewhere to get a drink. Visions of tall glasses of lager floated before his mind's eye. He saw the sign over a door in a wall, and the door led into a long room with a bar down one side of it, half-a-dozen glass-topped tables grouped about the other half of the room. The only customers were a silent, hard-faced trio at the end of the bar, who eyed him with curiosity. He ordered a lager, drank it down, and hurried back into the street.

He started walking again, his mind a restless turmoil of questions he couldn't answer. He took long strides and then his legs began to ache and he found a seat beneath a huge dark statue of Bismarck.

He felt relaxed, the tension in his mind and muscles slowly disappeared. He watched the people passing by along the pathway. He still seemed to be in the vicinity of the docks, the salty tang was still in the air. He felt higher up; beyond him were warehouses and crane tops, the masts of shipping and the river's far shore. He noticed how pretty some of the girls were with their flaxen hair and clear complexions. The men were dressed in their town clothes. There were offices nearby and the workers were going home.

It was getting late. Apart from the people hurrying by, there was a feel about the air. The Bismarck shadow was growing longer. He thought that a man passing seemed to notice him, and abruptly he stood up. He began to feel restless, he had to go on again.

The next thing he remembered, he was back at the hotel. He flopped down on the bed and fell asleep.

He awoke at precisely six-thirty. It was the same day he told himself vaguely. His shaven chin was still smooth. He'd slept no more than perhaps an hour. It was still warm, and he was too tired and the bed seemed to become more and more uncomfortable. Finally, about seven-fifteen, he stopped trying to sleep and he got up. He went into the bathroom at the end of the landing. His clothes were badly creased where he'd been lying in them.

He dragged his gaze from the wall mirror and the reflection that stared back at him with such probing curi-

F

osity, and he looked at the bath. Over the end of it was a shower. He decided he hadn't time for a bath and turned on the shower. He pulled off his clothes. When he had the spray running he kept adjusting the taps until he'd got the chill off the cold water; then he stepped under it. He'd brought the hotel towel from his bedroom and he was using their soap, but it didn't lather very well.

He towelled himself hurriedly. "You're not catching a train," he heard himself say. But he dressed as fast as he could and went downstairs. He couldn't keep still; had to keep moving. As long as he was going somewhere or doing something, he felt all right.

It was twilight outside. Overhead the reflection of the lights of the great city was already turning the sky into an orange glow. He walked through the dusk without any sense of direction or purpose. He must have headed straight for this bar along the dingy street. He went in, but it was so dark and dirty he came out again immediately. He went a little further, this thirst was coming on again. He came to another dive. There were pictures on the walls of the passage leading into the place of scantily-dressed girls and some wearing nothing at all. The lights in the passage were low.

The sound of voices drifted through from somewhere at the back. He could make out a shadowy staircase leading off the passage. A nasty-faced tout shuffled out of the shadows. His black-encircled sunken eyes between a broken nose glittered.

"Very good drinks, and beautiful girls for your entertainment."

Despite the thirst that urged him to go in to the bar, a nauseating feeling swelled up from the pit of his stomach. He suddenly rushed out into the street again, gulping in the cool air. He took long strides as if he couldn't get away from the place fast enough.

It was a long time before he found a suitable bar. It was quite a large place occupying a corner site and the entrance was glass-topped and above it the name was written in lights. The place was furnished on the borders of luxury.

Everything shone as though it had just been polished. After gulping down a couple of tall glasses of lager, he began to think about some place to stay the night. He felt tired, he wanted to rest his weary body. He found an hotel a few yards away from the bar. There were potted palms and easy chairs around the entrance-hall. He sat for a while in a comfortable chair by the window of his room. He began to feel hot and sticky again. He got up and stared out at the lights in the gathering dusk.

He tried to place himself; tried to break in from the outside. But it was no use. He went to the bathroom, turned on the taps and undressed. He took a long hot bath. He lay in the water, relaxing, but it was no more than a temporary lull. Within ten minutes he was out of the bath and dressing himself hurriedly. He was suddenly so hungry his head was spinning. He couldn't remember the last time he had eaten. There was a restaurant attached to the hotel; he went through an archway in the palm-ornamented hall.

He had spaghetti and a half bottle of dry Rheinland wine, which the waiter recommended. He felt better after that. The waiter brought him some coffee. But he drank no more than half a cup before he had the urge to be moving again. He paid his bill and went out into the street.

He just kept going until he saw a cinema and he went inside and bought a ticket. He was directed up a staircase. He found himself in a seat in the darkness. The film was about a big bank robbery. He sat through about half of the picture. He couldn't take any more.

He left the cinema, crossed the road, registering idly that the traffic drove on the right-hand side, and a few yards along, found a bar. He went inside knowing that that wasn't really what he wanted either. The time was pushing ten p.m.; but he wasn't interested in the time.

There weren't many people in the place. A few couples, a fat elderly woman with a little bald-headed man. Two young men, immaculately if somewhat over-smartly dressed. There were soft lights, and three alcoves in almost complete darkness where figures moved occasionally.

He stood at the end of the bar on his own, the half-empty glass of lager in front of him. He was smoking a cigarette, though he didn't remember buying any. The packet was lying on the counter. They were Camels, the cigarette tasted a little harsh, he thought. He had the feeling that he had been in the bar before, but he couldn't be certain. Then while he stood there it suddenly hit him that he had been aware all along that there was something wrong, that every now and then he'd stopped and wondered, but it hadn't really made any impression on him. But now an awful panic-packing feeling attacked him with jolting suddenness. He knew what had happened, what was wrong with him.

He didn't know who he was, or where he was, or what he was doing there.

Chapter Ten

Automatically Miss Frayle chewed the chewing-gum which the pretty blonde stewardess had given her. She had been given some for the take-off at London Airport, the stewardess explaining to her that she might experience a little deafness due to the strong change in atmospheric pressure as the airplane gained height. But if you swallowed, the sensation would quickly go, and chewing-gum made you swallow.

When they were coming in to land, Miss Frayle had remembered to press the bell-push beside her and asked for chewing-gum again; she had found it very nerve-calming. Besides, it seemed to her, you could get the deaf sensation descending as much as you could ascending, the changes in atmospheric pressure would be the same, only in reverse. Now she was repeating the same routine which she had gone through coming in and leaving Düsseldorf.

The illuminated sign ahead of her indicated they would be down at Hamburg-Fuhlsbüttel any moment; those passengers around her who had been smoking were putting their cigarettes out.

She sat next the window, the seat next to hers was unoccupied, for which she had been thankful. She found it easier to relax, keep her thoughts calm without someone else beside her. From the window she had seen the glow in the pale night sky above Hamburg. And as the Lufthansa twin-engined Convair 340 had eased its 255 m.p.h. to begin its circling preparatory to coming into land, she caught a glimpse of the Elbe and the lights of the docks. As the plane crossed the wide river the lights of the city took on a colourful pattern and she saw the waters of the two Alsters glisten below.

As the airplane had sped for Düsseldorf, first stop, she had eaten a deliciously cooked steak and sipped a glass of wine. She had felt better for the meal, the tension and anxiety had sapped her vitality. After coffee she had been unable not to feel thrilled when the good-looking Lufthansa captain had asked her if she would like to see what went on in the pilot's compartment. It gave her the same feeling of importance as when Inspector Hood had laid on the police-car to take her to London Airport. The word had obviously got around that she worked for the famous Dr. Morelle and was, therefore, regarded by Lufthansa as a V.I.P.

Glad to have her mind taken off her speculations about Dr. Morelle, she was fascinated by the vast array of instruments in the green-painted cabin; the papers covered with calculations, reference-books and official-looking forms, and the mysterious crackle from the loudspeaker which kept the aircraft in touch with ground control. She even relaxed sufficiently to allow the thought drift into her mind how ironic it was that the ruggedly handsome man, busily explaining the intricacies of the instrument-panel of this great machine bearing her from London across Europe, had not so very long ago flown a bombing-plane in the opposite direction.

At Düsseldorf there had been half-hour's wait while

she strolled around the brightly-lit airport buildings; then off again on the last leg of the flight for Hamburg.

And now Hamburg Airport lay directly ahead. The airplane's nose was down and the multi-coloured lights of the great runway were speeding upwards; and Miss Frayle was chewing away at her chewing-gum as hard as she could.

A chunky, very blond man with a light-grey trilby hat, pounced on her at the barrier as she came from the runway into the white stone reception-hall; there were nods and signs at the customs check and she found herself up some steps, down another flight of steps, and the blond man saying in excellent English: "You are Miss Frayle, I am Kriminalinspektor Graap."

In a moment she was in the long black police-car, a Mercedes-Benz 220 S, with a uniformed driver at the wheel, and moving off through the airport gates. "Have you heard anything—about Dr. Morelle?" she asked the chunky man beside her. Her heart sank as he shook his head.

She had managed to telephone Inspector Hood from London Airport before she left. He had no news about Dr. Morelle; his reassurance that she would find him safe and sound, with some perfectly good reason for his silence, had failed to comfort her. She had hoped that there would be good news to welcome her at Hamburg, but the plainclothes-man had only a straw of hope for her to grasp at.

"No news is good news," he said.

"You mean he is not on the list of the injured, or the —the killed?"

"*Jawohl.* We cannot tell for certain that Dr. Morelle

was on the Nord Express at the time of the crash; all those injured or killed have been identified."

She breathed a thankful sigh, and her eyes were moist behind her horn-rims so that she had to blow her nose.

Leaving Fuhlsbüttel behind the car turned down a number of side streets and then came to a wide road, on the other side of which was what appeared to be a park and then the glistening water of the Aussenalster. The detective told Miss Frayle that they were on Harvestehuder Weg and that the park on her left was comparatively newly opened, with a number of contemporary style statues. He was obviously extremely proud of Hamburg, which he said, was his birthplace.

Miss Frayle sounded as interested as she could, and stared out on her left at the lights reflected on the Alster and the brightly-lit ferry-boats going past. On her right were the lights of luxurious houses, with large gardens, some of which appeared to be clubs, they were so brightly illuminated. As they continued straight on now along the Alsterufer, the large white building of the U.S. Embassy loomed up, and new buildings which appeared to be offices.

Across the other side of the Alster, Kriminalinspektor Graap pointed out a large building with its name Atlantic Hotel in white lights high up. Then the car reached Neue Lombardsbrücke, a bridge with pleasing, modern lines. Then on across the traffic lights and under a railway bridge, past the old Lombardsbrücke on to Neuer Jungfernstieg.

Miss Frayle caught the reflection of lights and the shadows of spires on the Binnenalster, the smaller of the two lakes. Everywhere, lights, almost every building appeared to be lit somehow or other. On her right Shell House was lit in orangey-yellow. And then a few moments later the car stopped outside the Hotel Vier Jahreszeiten, which seemed to her to be one big blaze of light.

The commissionaire in a blue uniform hurried down the few steps up to the revolving doors of the hotel, and opened the car door for her. She went through the revolving doors, and crossed the thick, red carpet, to the circular reception-desk, behind which was another man in blue uniform. There were marble pillars and potted shrubs and she saw in the long windows, looking out on to the Alster, boxes of flowers. To the left of the entrance towards the grill-room were glass display-cases of jewellery and handbags. To her right were luxurious sofas and arm-chairs and small tables, with people having coffee, and beyond the swing glass doors, through which Miss Frayle could see the restaurant and waiters hurrying in and out.

While Miss Frayle signed the register an hotel porter appeared and took her suitcase. "Perhaps you would like me to wait for you, Miss Frayle?" Kriminalinspektor Graap said. "We can decide about plans for finding Dr. Morelle."

"I would like to talk to you more, in case there is anything we can think of that I can do to help."

"I will wait and we will have coffee," he said. "Don't hurry; you will want a rest for a little after your journey."

She smiled her thanks. She would like to relax for a little while; she wanted to fix her hair, change her dress, and at the same time she wanted to sort out her thoughts.

She had, she supposed, hoped sub-consciously that the mere physical fact of her arrival in Germany would result in her hearing good news; she had believed that the act of making the journey, of worrying and indulging in anxiety for Dr. Morelle's safety would in itself be sufficient to cause him to reappear, imperturbed and sardonically sceptical of her concern for him. "What you mean, my dear Miss Frayle," she could hear him saying in that silky-toned voice of his, "is that you were anxious to enjoy a little trip abroad to break the monotony of the important work in which you were engaged at Harley Street." It was like preparing for the worst and behaving accordingly, as an assurance that the contrary must therefore inevitably prevail. Like working yourself up to go to the dentist about an aching tooth and when you get there the ache has stopped.

The detective assured her that he would wait as long as she liked, or he would come back and see her. "I am entirely at your disposal." He gave her a little bow and she thought how good-looking he was, his blond straight hair above a sun-tanned face. His eyes were bright blue and his teeth when he smiled were very white.

"I will be twenty minutes," she said. She turned back as she followed the porter to the lift. Kriminalinspektor Graap stood there, stolidly muscular in his light double-breasted suit. She had caught his glance following her. She thought his eyes were not blue, after all, but a steely grey. Or was it because they were narrowed speculatively as they watched her? A sudden shiver of fear trickled down the back of her neck. She realized she was not in safe, dear old London. This was Germany. This was Hamburg, and though she didn't picture it as being as wicked as Paris, it was foreign, after all. And she hadn't got Dr. Morelle with her. And she couldn't phone Scotland Yard and Inspector Hood.

Out of the lift and along the wide corridor, with long mirrors on either side to her room. The porter went in and put her suitcase down on the stand at the end of the bed while she stood and gasped with pleasure. The porter grinned at her and pointed to the collection of bell-pushes by the door. "If you want something," he said in a strong accent. "Ring the bell;" and with another grin he was gone.

She noticed that each bell had a little figure beside it : a waiter; a maid; a uniformed porter. She turned to take in the room again; the long, green velvet curtains drawn across the two windows, their colour matching the thick green fitted carpet. The silk bedspread matched the light green frills on the white dressing-table; there was a leather-topped writing-bureau in the corner near the windows, with a chair in front of it; a small bedside table with a light similar to the one on the writing-desk and on the other side of the bed was a comfortable armchair.

Next to the white wardrobe with its long mirror was a narrow door, which Miss Frayle opened. It was a fabulous bathroom, completely tiled in pale green, the walls, the floor, the sides of the bath. The wash-basin was the same colour green, and the footbath; along the wall opposite the bath with its shower was a large heating rail; on the end wall a long mirror, in which she was reflected.

She thought she looked a little travel-weary and her nose was shiny. She went back into the bedroom and crossed to the windows. She pulled back the curtains, and the french-windows which opened on to two small balconies. They were double windows, the first one opened inwards and the second outwards. She stepped on to the balcony to look across Neuer Jungfernstieg directly below her, through the trees on the other side, to where the Alster reflected all the many colourful lights. From the restaurant came the murmur of dance-music, a waltz, dreamy and romantic. Miss Frayle sighed tremulously. If only she was here on holiday. A holiday with Dr. Morelle. At the thought, her mind switched to the blond detective downstairs and the grim realism of her being in this romantic hotel-room.

Quickly she ran a bath, while she unpacked the few things she had brought and transferred them to the wardrobe. Then she took a quick bath and changed into a plain but nicely cut frock. She brushed her hair and put on discreet touches of make-up.

She was giving herself a final glance in the mirror when she thought she heard a tapping noise outside the window. She had left the green curtains open, so that she could catch glimpses of the twinkling lights and glitter of water beyond the trees. She paused and stared in the direction from which she fancied the sound had come. She was deciding that it must have been the rattle of a drum in the dance-orchestra, when she heard the sound again.

It was a rap on the door. She crossed to it quickly, thinking that it might be the detective to say he was tired of waiting, and had come to hurry her up. As she was deciding that the blond, chunky man would hardly have come up to her room, but would have phoned her, and that therefore it must be a porter with a message, or perhaps the maid, she opened the door.

It was a porter; not the one who had come up with her in the lift, but another, younger man. He held out an envelope to her. "Miss Frayle?"

She opened the envelope and frowning behind her horn-rims read the note. It was written in a round, almost feminine hand-writing: "You are looking for Dr. Morelle. Go to Hagenbeck's Tierpark to-morrow midday. The Snake-house. I will speak to you there. Warning—Do not tell anyone. Your friend."

The young porter was watching her as she looked up at him, realizing he was still there. His expression was blank. She started to ask him who had given him the letter, then she remembered the warning in it and decided it might be best to ask no questions.

"There's no answer," she said and he turned away as she closed the door, re-reading the message.

Chapter Eleven

IT WAS like experiencing the sensation of looking into a mirror and there wasn't any reflection. That was what he felt like.

The man at the end of the bar stood there trying to think. His fingers curled round his glass, the Camel cigarette drooped from the corner of his mouth, its taste harsh as if he was unused to smoking the brand. He tried to think of the hotel-registers he'd signed, since he had been wandering round Hamburg after he had left the Hauptbahnhof that morning. He tried to remember the name he'd written.

Something like Bell or Bellamy? It wasn't a German name, he felt sure of that. He was equally sure neither of those two was his name. They didn't sound right.

He suddenly started to shake, his teeth began to chatter, saliva soaked hs cigarette-butt and he stubbed it out in the ashtray. He looked around. No one took any notice of him. Each had someone to talk to, the two over-smart young men were engrossed in each other's conversations; the little bald-headed man and the fat woman were talking as if there was no one else that mattered in the entire world.

He tipped his glass, but he didn't drain it. The lager didn't make him feel any better. He was still shaking. And he couldn't stand the bar any longer. He couldn't remember leaving but he was out in the street again, almost running.

It was like something was chasing him.

The next thing he remembered he was back in his hotel-room, turning out his pockets. He had gone through his note-case, but there was nothing in it, except the money. And he recalled obtaining that at the Hauptbahnhof. Or had he? There was nothing to indicate his identity. He didn't know if it was even his note-case, though there was something familiar about it, as if it had belonged to him. It was of crocodile-skin, expensive-looking and silk-lined and worn at the edges. There was no monogram on it. He took off his clothes and examined them. But there was no mark or name tag. His clothes didn't tell him anything.

He looked at the flat, gold watch on his wrist. That didn't tell him anything either, except the time. It was nearly ten-thirty p.m. He suddenly brushed the problem of learning identity from his mind. He was tired of trying to remember. He had a new idea. He decided he wanted to go to Bremen. Out of nowhere the name Bremen entered his thoughts.

He felt hot and sticky, so he took another shower. The towel was still damp from the shower he had taken earlier. He got dressed as fast as he could, stared at himself in the mirror, then hurried down and out of the hotel to the street. He walked quickly and then he stopped and asked a man who was walking with a woman on his arm the way to the station. Only he didn't go to the Hauptbahnhof. He went on to the Z.O.B., Zentral-Omnibus-Bahnhof, which was almost opposite the railway-station and was a long, low white building with a round tower. There were shops and coffee-bars inside for passengers waiting for buses which could take them anywhere all over Germany. There was a bus for Bremen just leaving; but he had doubts again now. He wasn't sure about going to Bremen, after all. Why should he go there? What had he got to do with Bremen? So he changed his mind and walked back through the city.

He found an all-night café in Mönckebergstrasse and drank a cup of coffee. He came out and walked on past the town hall and St. Michaelis' Church until he came to his hotel. There was no one in the hall. He went up to his room. He felt desperately tired; his legs ached and he wanted to sag at the knees. He undressed slowly and got into bed. He switched off the light.

But he slept no more than an hour. It was a dreamless sleep as if he were dead.

When he awoke the room was lit by greyish light. He realized that it was the glow of the street-lamps splashed on the ceiling. The rest of the room was gloomy with shadow. He felt terribly depressed. He didn't know what he was doing in Hamburg. He ought to have gone to Bremen, he told himself. But he couldn't think why. If he'd had a reason it was gone now. He got up and this time ran a warm bath in the hope that it would relax him. But he could not relax. He felt as jumpy and restless as before. As soon as he was dressed, he went out and started walking.

The night seemed stuffy; but he walked the streets until he was tired and aching. He found himself in the Reeperbahn, Hamburg's main street of night-spots, a long glittering row of seductive-looking signs and fronts lit up with multi-coloured lights and large photographs of alluring women. There was the Café Keese, where women ask the men to dance; the Menke, the name written in fiery red against a blazing background of white neons; Lausen, advertising its glamorous cabaret; and the Moulin Rouge with its nudes, and the cellar below with a Hungarian restaurant and a moustached violinist, playing romantic tunes to individual customers; there was the Zillertal, a big beer-hall with a Bavarian band and where customers were allowed to dance on the tables. At the end of the Reeperbahn was a side-street also given over to night clubs and pubs; also brothels and cinemas showing sex films called the Gross Freiheit. Beyond this street lay darker streets, the notorious area of St. Pauli.

He turned back half-way along Grosse Freiheit. He walked quickly, so that no prostitutes or pimps or touts accosted him. Every now and then he had that odd feeling that he was looking for something. He didn't know what it was; but the urgency of it was there, nagging at his mind. He felt thirsty again, that burning dryness in his throat. And he looked around for a bar. He was almost out of the Grosse Freiheit on his way back to the Reeperbahn. The sky above glowed like molten lead, it could have been broad daylight instead of night. He found a bar.

The entrance was a lighted doorway in a brick wall. Just inside were photographs of girls. There were glass doors and a uniformed figure nodded a welcome as he came out and opened the door. There was a blonde cigarette-girl chatting to a man in a dark suit. The girl wore a minute frilly skirt and fishnet stockings.

She gave him the eye as he passed her and went down some steps into the club which was hazy with the smoke of cigarettes and cigars. Everyone was packed closely round the small floor; on a dais a five-piece band played, and just to one side a curtained arch through which the cabaret-acts came out on to the floor. The walls glowed red from the lights in their scarlet shades, and tables had white telephones on which a customer could talk to other customers, or the hostesses.

He made his way to the small softly-lit bar in a recess, overlooking the dance floor. There was a young chap who looked like an American drinking and joking with a slant-eyed brunette. He bought himself a long, iced lager and took a look round.

The wall lights suddenly dimmed and a spot-light cut the darkness to catch a girl in the centre of the dance-floor. She had long auburn hair and an oddly delicate, heart-shaped face. Her teeth were white as her bright red mouth fixed itself in a smile. There was a nice figure under her filmy dress, and as the band went into the opening music the audience knew they were going to see more of it, much more. It was a strip-tease act.

She began taking off one skirt. There was another filmy skirt underneath, at least that was what it seemed like; and he realized that a light from the bar showed up his face. She could see him quite clearly. Each time she danced round she smiled at him, as he watched her over his glass. It was a nice smile. He kept on watching her until she had stripped down to the inevitable G-string. Then the spot snapped off and as the lights came up there was a long burst of applause. The girl had gone. She didn't come back to take a bow.

The band struck into a fast number and the floor was packed again. He was considering moving on, when the strip-tease girl appeared. She was wearing a provocative dress and she was at his side out of nowhere. He was so surprised, he couldn't believe she was speaking to him.

"I was watching you watch me," she said.

He couldn't answer her, he mumbled something and the barman waited expectantly for him to buy her a drink. It was the first time that anybody had even noticed him. It made him feel like a real person, that he belonged to the world after all.

The girl was smiling with her eyes now as well as her lips. She had deep brown eyes and although he knew she just wanted him to buy her drink, he didn't mind. He knew that was the whole idea, of course, but it didn't make any difference. It was worth it. She said she would have a scotch. A tall one, she told the barman. She turned to him.

"You looked lonely, I just had to come over." She had a marked American accent.

"I was," he said.

She talked to him about her act; did he like it and had he seen her before? She obviously took her work quite seriously; she wanted to build herself into something near the big-time. He did his best to appear interested, though all he could do was to wonder what he was doing here with this girl. Then she stopped talking; she sat there for a few moments, just looking at him. It was as if she hadn't really seen him before. "There's something wrong, isn't there?" she said.

It was the last thing he expected her to say. He couldn't believe she was the type to get worried about a casual stranger, a man who was there just to buy her a drink. Maybe she was a sentimentalist; the warmth in her smile really came from the heart He shifted uncomfortably.

"I'm fine," he said.

He brought out the packet of Camels. She took one

and he lit it for her. His hand was trembling. He could see her staring at it, and then she took his hand in hers. When he had lit his own cigarette, she said :

"What's on your mind?"

He began telling her then. Not all the story, but that he was lost, mentally and physically. He didn't know whether he expected her to believe him or not.

She kept shaking her red head and saying : "Oh, you poor thing." She made sympathetic murmurs in German. Her eyes were tender, her mouth softly curving. She couldn't have been more understanding if they had been old friends. It was unreal; he kept wondering where the snag was. He bought her another drink and one for himself.

"You should save your money," she said. She had glimpsed his note-case and the money in it. "You shouldn't be wandering around alone." She stared into face. "You don't want to be alone, do you?"

"You're being very kind to me," he said.

She touched his hand. "Will you wait for me?" she said. "I have to move around a little, make with the talk with some of the regulars. Then I do my act again. After, I'll be free as air."

He'd wait for her, he said. There was no hesitation in his answer. He watched her go round the dance-floor, singling out various men at the tables. He stayed where he was at the bar, smoking and drinking lager, impatient for her return.

He didn't see her again until she came on and went through her act. He realized that she possessed an attractive body. He watched her with interest; it still seemed incredible that she should have picked him out. He found it difficult to believe that anyone whose act made her appear so brazen, could be so sincere. It occurred to him that she moved with a grace and professional style that in itself was appealing, stripped or clothed. There was an air of innocence about her.

When she came back to him at the bar, all she wanted was some soda-water. "I don't take too much of the hard stuff. Have to think of my figure. It earns my living." Her name was Eva. She was billed as The Enchanted Eve, and the music she stripped to was the tune from the show, *South Pacific, Some Enchanted Evening*. He hadn't realized what the music was, he admitted to her. "That's because you were too interested watching me. Thank you for the compliment." She went on : "It's an idea to attract the Yanks," she said. "At first I thought you were one. Now, I know you're not."

They were speaking in German now; he said to her : "Because I'm speaking German?"

"You speak it very fluently," she said. "But it isn't only that. If you were a Yank you'd have tried to go to bed with me by now."

She began talking about him again. She was sure, she said, that if only he could rest and get a doctor, he would feel better; his memory would come back to him. "Where's this hotel you're staying at?"

He told her he didn't know the name of it. He couldn't remember the street, either; but he could tell her how to get there. He was sure he knew the way back to it. It was all right, he thought. Apparently he didn't sound over-enthusiastic.

"Maybe I could get you a room where I live," she said. "It's a quiet hotel. Very reasonable."

"All right," he said. He nodded towards the dance-floor. "How many more times did you say you have to undress before you go to bed?"

She giggled and put her hand affectionately on his arm. "I told you," she said. "I've given my last performance for to-night."

She clung to his arm as they went out of the place. It was just after one o'clock; he was surprised to learn that it was so late. He had no idea that he had stayed so long in the bar. It was the longest time he'd ever stayed in one place; he was grateful for that. All the same he felt glad at getting out in the air again, to be moving. He had used up all the sitting and talking he could take for a while.

They made their way quickly along the Reeperbahn, and turned left at the top, past Heiligergeistfeld, a large square of waste-land with trees on the edges. She was glad of the walk, she insisted, after the stuffy bar, and wouldn't let him hail a taxi-cab at the end of the Reeperbahn. He was still anxious to be moving, though she slowed his pace down. They went on down Glacischaussee, past Dammtor Station and along the Rothenbaum Chaussee, and she stopped outside a house, which like many others along the wide road, had been converted into an hotel. He waited in the semi-darkened deserted hall while she went through to find someone. She was back soon, her face unsmiling.

"There isn't a room," she said. "But there's one a few houses along. I'm sure you'll get fixed up there."

She put her arm through his and led him out and along the street. They came to a house which in the darkness appeared similar to the one where the girl had her room. A light burned in the hall and in one of the

ground floor windows flanking the front-door. Again
he waited in the hall while Eva vanished through a door
beside the reception-desk. After a few moments she re-
appeared with a tubby woman with straight grey hair.
He went towards them as the girl called out to him. His
eyes flickered over the cream-painted flight of stairs and
the doors either side while Eva said: "It is fixed. I will
take you up and you can see it."

The room was on the second floor front. It was comfortable and at once he longed to throw himself on the
bed and sleep. Weariness gripped him suddenly. Eva
was bouncing on the bed to demonstrate its springiness
for him. She would tell the woman downstairs he was
staying, she said. He nodded to her gratefully. She
seemed reluctant to leave as they stood at the door. "I'll
see you in the morning," she said.

He murmured his thanks to her for taking care of him.
His words sounded inadequate.

"I don't like leaving you," she said. She pressed close
to him in the doorway.

"I shall be all right." He fought to keep the utter
weariness out of his voice. She suddenly lifted her face
and kissed him on the mouth. Then she turned and closed
the door after her.

He stood staring at the door, listening to her high heels
tapping down the stairs, then her voice as she spoke to
the woman. He sat down on the bed. He knew that if
he had said it, she would have come back to be with him.
She wanted to, he was sure. He shook his head and then
he buried his face in his hands and keeled over on the bed.

That was the last thing in the world he felt like.

He fell asleep as he was.

Chapter Twelve

MISS FRAYLE took the No. 16 tram to Hagen-beck's Tierpark.

She had asked the blue-uniformed man behind Reception how to get there. He turned out to be something of an enthusiast and had eulogized the zoo's attractions to her at length. It was really a transit zoo, he explained; the great Hagenbeck would go off to Africa, returning with wild animals which were held until bought by other zoos or circuses. "No. 16 tram from Dammtor," the man at Reception had told her, "it will cost you one mark fifty to get in."

She had left the hotel at 11 o'clock allowing herself an hour in which to reach the rendezvous which had been given her so mysteriously. Walking briskly in the warm sunshine, she turned right at the end of Neuer Jungfern-stieg into the Colonnaden, seeing from the corner of her eye the elegant shops as she passed. In the shade of the colonnade, the windows gleamed from high-class tobac-conists exuding the aroma of cigar-smoke, to fashion-shops, enticingly displaying shoes and dresses. Miss Frayle found herself irresistibly making a mental note to spend some time window-shopping before she left Hamburg.

At the end of Colonnaden she paused at the busy cross-roads of Stephensplatz; remembering the directions she had been given, she waited for a green light on the

Esplanade, thronging with trams, other traffic and milling crowds, and crossed over, to turn down Dammtorstrasse.

On her right she passed a beer-garden, where the tables with their gaily striped umbrellas were set out beyond the low green hedge; people were already drinking coffee or beer. She went under Dammtor railway-bridge and crossed the road to the Strassenbahn Halteplatz, an island in the middle of the road. No. 16 was waiting. It comprised two long red and white cars; as she began to run for it, fearful that it would start without her, she saw the uniformed figure of the conductor glance at her. The tram-doors shut behind her and she bought her ticket from the conductor at his little desk.

It wasn't a bit like taking a bus from Oxford Street and she couldn't help thrilling to the novelty of it all as she sat on the wooden single seat on the left-hand side. She saw the green round dome of Hamburg University, glinting in the sunlight surrounded by well-kept lawns which stretched to the road. The tram was half full and as it clanged on its way, her thoughts were spinning round last night's events.

She saw again the young uniformed porter's blank expression as she took the note from him. *You are looking for Dr. Morelle,* it had said in that strange, almost feminine hand-writing. *Go to Hagenbeck's Tierpark tomorrow midday. The Snake-house. I will speak to you there. Warning—Do not tell anyone. Your friend.*

How she had stopped spilling it all to Kriminalinspektor Graap, she didn't know. She had gone downstairs, her heart racing as she put the strange message carefully in her handbag, to find him where she had left him, a patient expression beneath his blond straight hair, brushed back.

"You look so very much refreshed," he said to her, when she had apologized for keeping him waiting. "Quite well worth waiting for—if I may say so."

He had added this as if his compliment had gone too far, but his blue eyes had flickered over her appraisingly. Miss Frayle had blushed : he certainly was attractive, even if it did seem to her that there was something sinister about him. She supposed his accent added to his appeal, while at the same time she had tried to reassure herself that he was completely trustworthy, and that it was simply because he was foreign and she was far away from London, unable to turn to Dr. Morelle, that she felt slightly suspicious of him.

All the same she had not mentioned the note; but perhaps that had been on account of the warning it contained and her fear for Dr. Morelle's safety. But if it had been Inspector Hood and not this chunky blond sprucely-dressed Hamburg detective, she knew she would have told him without the slightest hesitation. She had asked him to have some coffee with her. The waiter had brought two large cups and she had watched fascinated as the detective helped himself liberally to the jug of cream.

Then he had pulled a copy of the *Hamburger Abend-blatt* from his pocket and handed it to her. It headlined the Nord Express smash. "All the injured and uninjured having been accounted for," he said, "our only conclusion must be that Dr. Morelle must have got off the train at Bremen. This we cannot know. In the inquiries we have been making, several of the restaurant-car and sleeping-coach staff say they saw him on the train just before it arrived at Bremen."

"But if he had got off at Bremen, for some reason, he would have heard about the crash. He would have got into touch with you."

"That is what one would expect."

Miss Frayle's gaze had dropped to the newspaper again. The Nord Express had left Bremen for the hour-and-a-half run to Hamburg, the last leg of its journey at 8.06 punctually. The express had been cleared outside Bremen; so far as the driver was concerned the next three mile section of the line was free. Having lost a couple of minutes at Bremen, the driver took the opportunity of making up time, deciding it was safe to increase speed. Thundering down the long incline the Nord Express had swept through wispy veils of mist on to the gentle curve where the double lines quadrupled with relief lines. It was on this stretch that the disaster overtook the train.

The signal-box controlling the first section of the relief lines had accepted a freight-train on the down main, but not until it had passed the points did the signalman concerned realize that some mental aberration had caused him to make a dreadful miscalculation; he should have diverted the freight to the relief line to await the passing of the express on the main.

Frantically he had telephoned the next box at the further end of the relief line asking him to stop the freight train and shunt it back on to the relief while he would hold up the express. He put the signals for the Nord Express at danger, but the signals were hidden by a swirl of mist at the crucial moment. The relief line

points, where the freight train had arrived to shunt backwards on to the relief were switched; the express jumped
the points as the guard's van of the freighter reached
them. The driver snapped his regulator shut and made
a full application of the vacuum brakes.

In the seconds before the great locomotive came to
rest at the side of the track a hundred and fifty yards
beyond the point of collision, the six-wheeled guard's van
practically disintegrated while the dozen trucks ahead of
it were destroyed beyond all recognition. The bodies and
frames of the first two Nord Express coaches left their
bogies and piled up against the engine tender, acting like
runners, so that the first and second coach leapt over
the locomotive and landed on their sides beyond. The
third climbed ten feet above the tender of the engine
which itself had been thrown up over a wrecked truck
carrying a load of steel, before ploughing down into the
embankment. The solid steel front of the engine's tender
saved the crew on the footplate and they escaped with
minor injuries and shock. But there was no trace of the
freight-train guard.

The leading bogie of the engine was pushed under
the trailing coupled wheels, one bogie wheel having been
torn from its axle at a shearing force of some seventy
tons. There was no fire and, apart from the coaches
immediately involved, there was no telescoping. In the
second half of the train there were few injuries to passengers, for these coaches did not leave the metals.

The force of the impact thrust the freight train forward some seventy yards. The driver and fireman were
injured, but the driver managed to drag himself along
the line to warn the signal-box so that all other traffic

entering the section could be stopped and the rescue services alerted.

Miss Frayle had chewed at her lower lip. Now that she had a clear picture of the accident, the absence of news of Dr. Morelle had become more sinister in her mind. But if she was certain that he had not been among the casualties, she was also unable to understand why he had got off the train at Bremen. Why hadn't he contacted the Hamburg police, or someone else who had his confidence to advise them of his intentions?

Draining his coffee cup and folding up the newspaper, Graap had eyed her sympathetically. "There is nothing more to tell you; nothing more you can do to-night except get some sleep. You must have had a very exhausting day. From what we know of your Dr. Morelle, he can take care of himself and has good reasons for his actions. Even if they are a little worrying to others."

She had given him a wan smile. She was just a little bit flattered by the way he had referred to Dr. Morelle; she had never before imagined him as *her* Dr. Morelle.

"The moment we have any news, we'll inform you at once," the detective had told her. She had watched him leave the hotel, horribly unsure if she had done the right thing by keeping the letter back. A few minutes later she had gone thoughtfully upstairs to her room.

Oddly enough Miss Frayle had fallen asleep as soon as her head touched the pillow; it was a dreamless sleep, so far as she could recollect. She ought to have turned and twisted, clutching at the bedclothes as she lived through violent dreams in which she was searching for Dr. Morelle among that terrible train-wreckage.

But she had slept beautifully.

Awaking, still drugged with sleep she had been startled and annoyed to find it much later than she had expected. Dimly she remembered someone coming into her bedroom with morning tea which she had ordered. But the tea was cold. She must have fallen asleep again without realizing the time. She had bathed and dressed quickly and gone down to breakfast. It was ten o'clock.

Miss Frayle had been unable to do more than manage toast and coffee; her approaching appointment had taken away all her appetite. She went out of the restaurant and hovered about the hotel-foyer, undecided, watching a porter loaded with baggage follow what looked like a honeymoon couple. The red-headed girl looked very happy, she gazed up with adoration at the man, and he had his arm around her waist as they went out to a waiting taxi. Miss Frayle reflected inconsequentially how comforting it was to glimpse a little happiness in the midst of so much violence and anxiety.

Presently she had sat down facing the glass doors. She picked up an illustrated magazine and began to turn the pages, glancing without much interest at the pictures; it was a German magazine and she couldn't read the captions. Every movement that caught the corner of her eye had brought her head up, though she didn't know whom she was expecting exactly. Or was it that blond chunky figure she was awaiting to appear? It wasn't until now, as she sat in the clanging tram with the conductor's voice over a microphone announcing the stops, that she realized it was Kriminalinspektor Graap she had been waiting for.

And then : "Good morning, Miss Frayle." He was standing there, smiling down at her; and she hadn't noticed him come in at all. He was in the light grey suit and carried his soft grey hat in a square, sun-tanned hand. The way his clothes sat on him gave Miss Frayle the impression that he was all muscle. The type of man it was comforting to have on one's side, she thought; and yet again it was on the tip of her tongue to tell him all about her trip to Hagenbeck's Zoo, or Tierpark, or whatever it was called.

But she didn't say it.

"No news," he said. He gave a slight shrug of his square, thick shoulders. "Personally, I am convinced that Dr. Morelle is lying low for reasons of his own; that he has deliberately taken advantage of the tragic accident to throw someone off the scent, or some similar manœuvre."

She had nodded. "I am sure you are right. It is not unlike him to act in this way."

"I am glad you are not allowing yourself to become desperately anxious," he said. "If I can make this waiting easier for you, then please allow me. If you intend to go out, would you like someone to go with you?"

She had glanced at him sharply.

But his blue eyes were wide and unsuspicious; his serious face was bent on her in a kind, protective way. She felt sure he had no inkling of her intended appointment. And yet was there a certain tenseness about his attitude, a watchfulness in his manner, which his eyes belied? Over her horn-rims she stared at him. His expression remained the same. Even the obvious start she had given at his question seemed to have passed unnoticed by him.

"Thank you so much," she said, striving to be careful not to arouse suspicion. "You know, I don't mind being alone." She had adjusted her glasses which really needed no adjusting. "I've heard so much about Hagenbeck's Zoo, I've been thinking of going along to see it. I shall be back here for lunch, of course."

He nodded approvingly. "I am sure you will enjoy it. I, too, have heard so much about the zoo, though I have never been near the place; and I am born here."

"Isn't that funny," Miss Frayle had said. "I've never been to the Tower of London. And I was born there. London, I mean, not the Tower."

"Perhaps it's because I see so much of the jungle in my job," he said. He had moved away abruptly, as if afraid that what he had said had frightened her, or annoyed her. "I will call again at lunch-time." He had glanced at her, a curious gleam in his eye. "You will please mind how you go."

"I'm sure I shan't get attacked by a lion," she said.

He said nothing, but the look he wore was not optimistic, so that she had to smile at his concern as she watched him go out of the hotel, and she had wished she could have told him of the real reason for her visit to the zoo.

The tram-ride took some twenty-five minutes and then it had reached the crest of a slight hill, and she saw the trees and rocks above the high wall; this was Hagenbeck's Tierpark. Somewhere beyond the wall a lion was roaring, and Miss Frayle could not repress a slight shiver of apprehension. Then she was paying her one mark fifty at the turnstile at the main gate. She turned right along the dirt path; the man at the turnstile had directed her to the Snake House. The time by her wrist-watch was thirteen minutes to midday. She was in good time.

It was not very busy, for which she was grateful. Having to shove her way through crowds of sightseers and noisy children would inevitably have caused her to reach the same conclusion she had reached on her last visit to the Zoological Gardens in Regent's Park : that it was not the animals but the human beings who seemed to be behind the bars.

Miss Frayle passed the elephants in their life-like enclosure. A large ditch surrounded the elephants, who moved amongst trees and old trunks; and there were water-holes and rocks. The monkeys were enclosed in a natural state : rocks and caves, trees and water-holes beyond a wide ditch and then a wall and railings through which the public could watch.

Miss Frayle continuing along the path divided by flower-beds, with cranes and storks on one side, reached the Snake House.

She went into the greenish, shadowy, warm atmosphere and made her way slowly round the glass-fronted enclosures. Here was an alligator tank, and she regarded the greenish-grey inanimate shapes lying round the pond. One was entirely submerged beneath the pond's surface except for the tip of a wicked-looking snout.

She glanced about her. The place was almost deserted. There were two figures, a man and a woman farther along, and a very old man with bent shoulders, walking towards the steps at the other end. Miss Frayle saw no sign of anyone who looked as if they might be the writer of the note. Her watch said just on twelve o'clock. She walked on, giving only a brief glance at the chameleons, the pythons lying intertwined in moist, shining coils, and the beady-eyed lizards.

It suddenly occurred to her that it might not be a man who had written her. She had assumed it was, but it could be a woman; the handwriting wasn't a man's, for a start. Somehow the idea that it was a woman seemed more menacing. Her heart was racing, and then as she stopped and eyed with compulsive disgust a cobra flattened against the front of its glass case, the voice seemed to sound in her ear.

"Miss Frayle?"

Her heart jumped, she felt sure it had stopped, then it raced again as she turned slowly to face the owner of the voice.

Chapter Thirteen

About the time Miss Frayle was having breakfast at the Hotel Vier Jahreszeiten, the girl, Eva, had made her way along Rothenbaum Chaussee to the café she regularly used. She seldom ate breakfast, and this morning she had felt disinclined even to make coffee in her own room. She decided to slip into the café for a few minutes, and then go along to see how the man had made out.

She was curious about him, wondering who he was and how he came to be wandering around Hamburg alone, and St. Pauli at that. She didn't know what to do about him. What kind of way did you handle anyone who'd lost their memory?

She didn't know why she had first been attracted to him. She knew herself for a sentimental fool, all right. She wanted to take care of him the same as she would have wanted to take care of a stray cat. Only there was more to it than that. He wasn't exactly a stray character; and there was something about him that appealed to her. He appealed to any woman, she thought. He was no tramp; he was well-educated, that was obvious.

But it wasn't this which had drawn her to him at the drop of the hat. And it wasn't only that he must have attracted her because he had looked such a lonely figure.

She knew she was a push-over for anyone who seemed lonely.

But she felt way out of her depth with this one. Over her coffee she decided on a line of action. Unless she did something about him he'd just go on drifting until his money ran out. She made up her mind to persuade him that morning to go to a hospital or a doctor.

She was stirring her coffee absently, her eyes on the morning paper the man opposite was reading. The front page had something about a train smash. But she was thinking about the man and how much she wanted to see him again. There was a phone-box a few yards along, past the café, she knew. On an impulse she got up and went out.

She found the yellow kiosk and went inside. She dropped the phennigs into the coin-box and picked up the telephone.

When it shrilled in the hall of the house, the man was at the foot of the stairs, a newspaper clutched in his hand. He had awakened at half-past eight. He had refused breakfast; he had drunk several cups of coffee and then he had gone out to buy a paper. The sudden ring of the bell had startled him.

He made a move as if to answer the phone, and then drew back. But something made him stay long enough to see the tubby, grey-haired woman pick up the phone, and then he went slowly upstairs. Before he got far the woman at the phone called to him.

"It's for you," she said.

He stared at her disbelieving. It was then he remembered the girl last night. The ringing had stirred his sluggish memory. He decided it must be her. He could remember her name. Eva. And that dump where she worked. It must be her, it must be Eva. It couldn't be anyone else. He didn't know anyone else in town.

"Hello?" the man said into the mouthpiece.

"How are you this morning?"

It was the girl, all right.

"About the same," he said. "I don't expect to get right overnight. But you have been very kind, and I'm very grateful."

"Grateful enough to see me again?"

"Why not?" But he had hesitated. "What time?"

"Just when you're ready."

He was silent for a moment; then he said: "In about an hour?"

"Okay," she said. "Be round then." She hung up.

He put down the receiver and stood silently in the hall, wishing he'd said he couldn't see her. But he didn't want to hurt the girl over the telephone. She had been very sweet to him.

He went out and found a flower-shop and bought her a mass of flowers, white flowers. He didn't know what they were called, but they had a subtle scent. He took them along to where she lived, and left them with a card thanking her for everything. He didn't go back to his place; he didn't want all the explaining to the tubby woman, and he was scared of running into the girl. He went off along Rothenbaum Chaussee, and at once he seemed to breathe more freely. He was very grateful to the girl, but he'd had enough. She was beginning to make him uncomfortable.

He never expected to see her again.

But he was wrong about that.

He set off quickly along the street. He'd begun to tremble once more. But if he kept moving he would shake it off. But there was another sensation which was more wearing to his nerves. There were so many people, and the streets were too narrow, he felt suffocated and hemmed in. He began to get panicky. And that was the last sensation he remembered for a long while. He kept on walking. He must have done that.

When he began remembering again he found he was all alone on a path at the south end of a park. Then he was walking again until he came to a lake in the middle of the city. He began to walk round it. He passed an expensive-looking hotel and he thought there was something about it that appealed to him. He reached the corner and stopped. He turned round and came back. There were people going in and out, and he stood there and watched them.

Then he moved again, walking back and forth and hanging around the hotel-entrance and watching the people, until the commissionaire in blue uniform noticed him and gave him a suspicious look. But he was reluctant to lose sight of the hotel. Only he couldn't stay there with that tall, uniformed figure watching him. The next time he reached the corner, he kept going. All the time it seemed he was made conscious of the huge buildings in plain, heavy brick architecture, and the equally distributed windows, oblong glass eyes; all a uniform beauty harmonizing with the northern sky.

Turning off into a side-street, he continued along it until he came to a bar. The thirst hit him again. It was a small place with pictures of prize-fighters around the walls. It was midday, and the place was empty except for the barman, polishing the glasses. He had the radio on, playing waltzes. The man drank a lager and went out. He walked around a couple of blocks, and then somehow he found himself back at the hotel he'd been staying at before he'd gone along to that place and met Eva. There were the potted plants and the easy chairs in the hall.

He bought himself a newspaper and he went into the hotel and sat down near the door and read the newspaper. A lot about some train smash. He began thinking about Bremen, and once more he experienced the urge to go there. Instead he went into the hotel restaurant and ordered a meal, everything he could think of. His stomach felt so empty it hurt. But when the food came he couldn't eat. He was too tired and restless. The waiter who had served him the previous evening was quite distressed.

"You look ill," he said. "You should rest."

There was no one in the hall except the clerk behind Reception who gave him the key to his old room and nodded cheerfully to him as he went upstairs. He got to his room and flopped on the bed.

He began remembering a tunnel and climbing a long flight of steps, and an empty street. It felt dark, oppressive. There were hardly any people about. There wasn't even a car or a truck going by. Then other streets came up into his consciousness. He was walking through them; and one of them came out at a railway-yard. Everywhere tracks and freight-cars. He walked for about a mile alongside a high wire fence. He began looking for a way out, but the fence went on. He kept going with it. Then he came to some old box-cars and junk blocking the way, and he lost the fence. He ended up back in the middle of the yard again, the freight-cars a dark mass all round him. There came the rumble of trains, crossing the iron-work of bridges and he guessed that it was traffic over the Norder Elbe. He started climbing under the cars and over the couplings, trying to get out that way.

But there wasn't any way out. He was hemmed in. Trapped.

He remembered that he tried to run and couldn't. He didn't have the strength. His legs were weak, he felt cold and sick. He must have crawled underneath a car, he seemed to wake up with a start, and there was the box-car above him and he was cramped and aching stretched across the sleepers. Then he heard somebody coming. It was a man, who looked like a railway-official. The man saw him and started yelling, but he was already coming out. The watchman was suspicious at first, but he led the man down the tracks a few hundred yards to an open gate and a street.

He went out of the gate and down the street, until he came to some buses. One of them was half-full and ready to leave so he jumped on. But after only a short distance, he got off the bus and without knowing how he did it, he made his way back to the hotel.

There was some kind of a party going on in the restaurant. He could see the people talking and laughing and drinking. Everyone looked very happy. He sat where he could watch the people enjoying the party, and he felt very lonely. It was worse than walking the empty streets. And all of a sudden he couldn't stand it, and he went up to his room.

He felt dreadfully muzzy, everything seemed out of

focus. Sometimes he wondered if he'd lost his glasses, though he'd never remembered wearing any. He moved restlessly about the room and kept peering out of the window. It was a nice day. The sky was blue with wisps of cloud. The sun was warm.

That awful, helpless feeling flooded him. He felt hunted. Bremen came into his thoughts. Suddenly the only thing he could think of was to get to Bremen as quickly as possible. That meant the train. He hurried out of his room and downstairs and on to the street as if he had only a few minutes in which to catch the train. He got to the Hauptbahnhof. He remembered it as the place where he had first come alive; but he couldn't recall when it was. It might have been yesterday; it might have been ten years ago.

He had lost all sense of time. Now once more he stood at the top of the wide, grey stone steps above the platforms where the people milled. He tried to get his bearings, as if by returning to the scene he might find something which would put him in the path back to normality. He might learn who he was and where he came from. All that happened was that he turned past the bookstall with its glossy magazines and newspapers and made for the booking-office.

He bought a ticket and got on to the platform and into a train that was due to leave for Bremen in a few minutes. But just before it was about to start he began to feel uneasy. He was alone in the carriage and he was afraid that the idea of going to Bremen was a mistake; there was some danger about it. He couldn't sit there worrying, he couldn't stand being in the compartment alone.

He got out of the train and watched it pull away from the platform. He began to hurry off the platform, up the steps and out of the station. He was back outside the rich looking white hotel once more with what he knew now was the Binnen Alster, its waters sparkling in the sunlight, behind him. Out of the corner of his eye he saw someone come out on one of the small, green-painted balconies on the second floor. He saw people going in and out of the shops below to the right of the hotel. He stood where he could see the glass revolving doors and kept looking at the faces appearing and disappearing as if there might be one he knew. The commissionaire was so busy opening car and taxi doors, he didn't notice him this time.

It was one-thirty-three by his wrist-watch. For the first time it occurred to him that the flat, thin gold watch was expensive and he wondered how he had come by it. He eyed it thoughtfully for a little while.

He must have stood there quite a time. Because finally he couldn't hold out any longer; whoever it was he expected to see there wasn't going to appear. He turned away and started back to his own hotel, the one he'd gone back to that morning. But now he'd forgotten the name of it, and where it was and what it looked like. There seemed to have been so many hotels he had stayed at.

He turned back past the huge statue of Bismarck, and down Holstenwall. When he reached the end of Gorch Fock Wall he turned off left towards Dammtor station and then he found himself on a short road, at the end of which was Planten un Blomen exhibition park. He paid at the turnstile and went in.

He sat down on a long wooden bench and tried to think, but he couldn't. His mind was dead. He was too miserable and he began to get the shakes again. A couple of children went by, hand in hand. They smiled at him, but he didn't take any notice. The fountains sparkled and were enveloped in a multi-coloured mist in the sunlight.

His gaze wandered across the grass and through the trees. He saw a uniformed park-keeper standing by a little confectioner's. There was a girl nearby with a pram. She was buying a large ice-cream. The park-keeper smiled at the baby in the pram and spoke to the girl. Then he moved along the path towards the man on the bench, who now dragged himself up and went to meet him, as he approached. He suddenly wanted to talk to somebody.

The park-keeper was very polite; he thought he was dealing with a drunk and behaved as if trying to humour him. But after they'd talked a few minutes, the keeper moved off. The man stood there a little while, and then walked slowly to the turnstile.

As he passed through them a sudden, urgent voice stopped him.

"We've been looking for you everywhere."

It was Eva; there was a man with her.

Chapter Fourteen

At precisely fifty-six minutes past one o'clock that same afternoon the telephone rang in the house which stood on a corner on the Elbchausse, six miles outside Hamburg on the way to Blankenese. A long, low, white house with a white pillared porch framing the wide entrance doors reached from the front drive by broad green tiled steps. It stood in an extensive immaculately kept garden, surrounded by a high white brick wall.

Heavily-timbered gates opened on to the Elbchausse itself; more gates opened on to the side-road, across which was a park, its lawns and ornamental lakes screened from the road by rhododendron bushes and trees.

The white house had two garages, one either side and adjoining the main building; each had part of the upper rooms above them. One garage housed a sleek blue Mercedes-Benz, model 300 de luxe convertible, the other a rakish 300 SL model two-seater roadster. Both garages had doors giving access to the house and garden.

The back of the house faced the Elbe which bounded the garden, steep to the edge of the river, which was tidal and three hundred yards wide; a straight stretch of dark water, its distant bank flat reclaimed marshland built over with houses and dock-structures.

The wide white-pillared veranda ran the width of the back of the house, the ground floor french-windows opening on to it from three large rooms. From the veranda three sets of steps led down to the lawn, beyond which paths and more steps led through a rockery and across another square of lawn to the boat-house, over which hung old willow-trees. The boat-house was large, part timber and park brick. It could also be reached by an underground tunnel leading from the cellar of the house. A short jetty stuck out from the bank alongside the boat-house, and a blue and white speedboat lay tied up. It was a sixteen foot Avenger, built by the British Aqua-craft company and powered by 65 b.h.p. Venom engine. She was a four-six seater of sleek modern design, with the top line of her hull rising in tail fins at the stern.

The white house and all the set-up suggested the residence of some wealthy Hamburg tycoon, or banker. It was in fact, Leon Stierlin's headquarters; and it was he who answered the phone. It was on his private extension on which only he ever took or made calls.

Next to the room in which he was speaking quickly into the mouthpiece was the pink and gold bedroom overlooking the gardens and the Elbe, and Winsome Deans sat at the gilt-edged dressing-table mirror indulging herself in her favourite occupation; she was studying her reflection. She wore a billowy *négligé* over her scented body and the soft, creamy skin it revealed met with her full approval. She was proud of her body; she was quite crazy with admiration for her long slender legs, the smooth curves of her hips and tiny waist and the firm, full breasts; almost as crazy about them as the things they brought her; the home-comforts, the cash.

She reckoned she had been pretty lucky. Travelled everywhere first-class, had everything she wanted and more. She had never had it so good as now; and yet it was only recently that the little niggling fears and worries had started up in her mind. She imagined that even the girl-friend of the most powerful racketeer in Europe had to take the rose-coloured spectacles off once in a while. She only knew he was in the racket, the dirt, the violence; she didn't see what went on, what brought all the cash in; she had ideas about some things that chilled her insides, but there was nothing she could do about it.

She leaned closer to the mirror to straighten the little worry lines beneath her eyes. She knew what was bothering her a trifle. It was the girl who had been brought to the house after the Nord Express smash-up. She had worried within herself wondering what Leon had in store for this girl. She was some danger to him, that was why she was kept in the cellar; and that something dreadful would happen to her Winsome Deans felt pretty sure. She had seen that look on Leon's suave face before, when something had come unstuck; when someone got taken care of. She sighed. This was where the cash and having it so good lost some of its gloss around the edges.

Maybe she was getting too much of a conscience. She started to fix her face, and tried to put such things out of her mind. This conscience idea was ludicrous.

She stood before the wall mirror near one of the two large rounded windows, and slipped off her *négligé*, admiring the reflection; then she went over to the double wardrobe, its deep walnut doors surfaced with a filigree pattern of gold and silver, and selected a plain, dark dress from the huge collection inside.

In the other room Stierlin had hung up on the phone conversation. The door leading from his room, his office, which was furnished in a surprisingly restrained style, dominated by an enormous writing-desk and filing cabinets, to the bedroom was sound-proofed. So was the door opening on to the staircase. He opened this door noiselessly as Winsome Deans came out of the bedroom, and he watched her descend the white staircase. She didn't see him.

The sun was shining through the tall rounded window above the hall-doors, its rays glittering on the chandelier suspended from the ceiling over the centre. The reflection of its light dazzled her momentarily, she moved across the parquet floor, her eyes flickering over the oil paintings on the cream walls. They were pastoral scenes, peaceful landscapes.

She passed the gaily-patterned Japanese screen, and knew why she scowled suddenly to herself. Behind the screen was the door that led to the cellar. She had only been through it once. She remembered the short passage and the thick heavy door at the end, and the stone steps down into the earth. And then the final door. She snapped off the thoughts in her mind, and moved to the double-doors facing her. She opened them and went into the library.

The three tall windows reached from floor to ceiling. Books lined the walls in their oak shelves. Leon had boasted to her that he had not read one of them. He read the newspapers, French, German, English and American; he read the long letters in code; that was about the extent of his reading. She swung round at a movement behind. She hadn't heard Leon come into the room. It was a trick of his, walking quietly and the wall-to-wall carpet was expensively thick and sound-absorbing.

"I'll be lunching here, *chérie*," he said.

She pouted, and used a four-letter word.

He shrugged. "Just had a phone-call and I'm expecting someone."

She immediately thought of the girl in the cellar. She guessed the visitor would be something to do with her. "I get it," she said slowly. "So I'll eat here, too. Okay?"

"Okay, *chérie*, if you want."

She picked a cigarette from the silver casket, and lit it with the desk-lighter. There was something tense about Leon; he wasn't often this way. That nagging fear caught at her mind again. She dragged quickly at her cigarette.

"What about that brunette in the cellar?" She made it sound conversational, but she was aware of the narrowed look he gave her. She hardly ever asked him any questions about the racket.

"She may be able to help me," he said, slowly and without emotion. "A little experiment. Scientific sort of thing. Over your head. Forget it, will you?"

He was at the antique Chippendale cabinet. When he opened the door the glint of bottles and glasses flashed into the room. She wanted to ask him more questions, only she was nervous about it. What was this stuff about a scientific experiment? Leon wasn't interested in space-travel, or anything.

"Gin?" he said to her. "Give you that appetite you're worrying over."

She nodded, and he filled the two glasses and took one to her. He put his face close to her cheek. He tried to kiss her on the mouth but she turned away. He raised a heavy eyebrow at her.

"I'm a bit edgy, I guess."

"Take a car and go out for a long drive," he said over his drink.

"So you want to get rid of me, is that it?" she said lightly. His teeth were bared in a white smile. His teeth looked a little too perfect, every one was an expensive capping job. He didn't say anything. She knew he thought she was kidding. "No," she went on, "I'll stick around. But I'll keep out of your hair."

"You do just that," he said. And for a heart-chilling moment she wondered if he did think she was kidding or not.

The time was two-fifteen when they had lunch at the long table in the large room whose french windows opened on to the terrace. The sunlight filled the garden and the river beyond looked less dark and grim. Leon was less chatty than usual and they sat silent over coffee and smoked. He turned the pages of the newspapers. She tried to fix her attention on the fashion-magazines. But she kept lifting her head to Leon, who seemed to be listening for something.

It was two forty-five when the sound of a car brought him to his feet and he went out into the hall, Winsome following. He turned to her; his face was taut and expectant.

"I'm going up to hit the sack," she said.

Winsome stood back from the staircase until she was concealed by the corner of the corridor leading to two of the bedrooms and the bathroom. She could just glimpse the front of the hall below.

Two men came in, one young, heavily-built, hat over his eyes; he was holding the arm of a tall, gaunt man. There was a brief conversation between the first man

I

and Leon in German. The other man seemed dazed, lost. A great wave of pity for him swept over her. Then the three of them moved out of her line of vision; she heard a door open, the door behind the Japanese screen, she guessed. It closed dully. There was silence.

She knew that they had gone down to the cellar where the big, dark girl was kept prisoner. She wouldn't have known anything about her, that she was in the house at all except by chance; she and Leon had been returning from Hamburg in the Mercedes late in the morning of the day before and another car was in the drive. The young heavily-built man she had just seen and another slim dark man were taking the girl into the house. She didn't want to go. The first man had caught her a thud over the ear with a curious chopping blow and they'd had no more trouble with her. Leon hadn't said a word or moved a muscle, just sat there at the wheel. But it was obvious to her that the trio's arrival wasn't entirely unexpected by him. A little later she had recalled where she'd seen the slim, dark man before. Paris; she'd met him once and very briefly with that bent cop, Inspector Rommerque.

Leon had made no comment about what she'd seen. He hadn't said for her to pretend it hadn't happened, or anything like that. But she knew she wasn't meant to talk about it, not even to him too much. And not at all to anyone else.

Her mind fastened on the man who'd been brought here, who looked desperately lost. She thought his gaunt figure and aquiline features would haunt her for the rest of her life, as she went on upstairs to the pink and gold bedroom.

Chapter Fifteen

THE DOOR hidden by the Japanese screen closed with
a heavy muted sound behind them, and the man found
himself bunched between the thick-shouldered individual
who had brought him in the car, and the other, who
had a purposeful air, whose mouth snapped cruelly as
he gave the orders.

The passage sloped fairly steeply, so that he had difficulty sometimes in not slipping; his knees were already
buckling from the hours upon hours of walking he had
done. But now to his exhaustion of spirit and physical
weariness was added an awareness of approaching peril.
He knew that somehow he had stepped into a trap.
Neither man at his elbow had said anything to him, beyond a muttered caution to keep his head down on
account of the low ceiling, but each of them exuded
menace.

He still couldn't understand it; he had no idea what
the reasons were for his being where he was; or to whom
he'd been brought. Eva and the man had found him
by the turnstile of Planten un Blumen. They had gone
into a café, and he had been persuaded to see a doctor.

"A special sort of doctor," the powerful-shouldered
young man had said.

Eva had to leave them together, she had a rehearsal at
the club. Before she went she had begged him to listen
to the other's advice. And so he had finally got into the

young man's car; and this was the result. He didn't remember the drive out to this house. The car had been very fast.

The suave individual who had been awaiting them had held a hurried conversation with the man who'd brought him, but he hadn't asked him who he was, or what he was doing. Not that he could have answered the questions. He wished he could have told him anything he wanted to know. Nothing seemed to make sense. And now he was led along this dimly-lit passage without any explanation. All he could decide was that he'd been tricked into coming here for some strange reason.

He wondered if Eva had realized what was going on. Somehow he didn't believe she had. He seemed to remember her giving the impression that the man with her at Planten un Blumen was only an acquaintance, she'd met that morning for the first time. He was on his left side now as the three of them went down and down into the earth, the light from the bare electric-bulbs spaced evenly in the ceiling harsh and cold. The man on his left still kept his hat-brim shading his eyes. He had worn the hat in the café and in the car.

They came to a heavy iron door which the sleek dark man unlocked and they went through and down a flight of stone steps. There was another door. The click of a light switch, the door was opened and they were in a large cellar, concrete-floored, with reinforced pillars supporting the low roof, which gave the impression of splitting the place into several smaller rooms. There was a wooden trap-door in the wall on the further side, a large galvanized tank fitted into a recess, and opposite a long, wooden bench, on which a big, dark-haired girl lay, staring at them and blinking in the bright light. The atmosphere was cold and dank, claustrophobic.

The man realized that he was being forced with his spine against one of the pillars opposite the tank, his arms wrenched behind him round the pillar and his wrists tied. Everything was happening very quickly, so that his mind seemed able to register only part of what was going on; in any case he was too exhausted, too weak to resist. He experienced the sensation that he was watching it all happening to someone other than himself. He couldn't believe that he was personally involved. He suddenly remembered his bedroom at the hotel at which he'd last stayed; his thoughts dwelt on the room and he was quite convinced that he would awake very shortly to find himself back there, stretched out on the bed. Then he would rush out, he supposed, and start off on that interminable walking round the city.

A phantasmagoria of the streets reeled dizzily through his mind. The streets, the milling crowds, the advertising-signs, the shops and hotels; the clubs and bars. Eva, he thought, where was she now? Was it possible that she had betrayed him? He thought of the flowers he had left for her at the house on Rothenbaum Chaussee.

Obeying the other's order the man in the hat had pulled the girl to her feet. Her hands were tied behind her.

"Look at her."

He did not realize that he was being spoken to; then the dark sleek figure was at his side and had pushed his chin back with a savage thrust so that the back of his head slammed into the pillar against his spine.

The dark man unloosed a flow of obscenities. "Look

at her," he spat out. "You recognize her; you know who she is."

He shook his head painfully.

"We shall see." The other swung on the girl. "You know him."

She stared back at him, her eyes above her high cheek-bones flashing defiant hatred. The heavy-bodied man was gripping her about her arms.

"I have never seen him before."

She answered him in French, the language in which he had spoken to her. The man holding her released his grip to slap her with the back of his muscular hand across her face, leaving a livid streak there. "You were together on the Nord Express," he grated through large white teeth, his French had a strong German accent.

She said nothing.

The sleek man said in a soft voice: "You refuse to identify him, eh? And he can't identify himself. Maybe we will bring back his memory."

He produced a small leather-covered case from his pocket, out of which he took a hypodermic syringe. It gleamed in the electric-light. He stepped forward and while the other held the struggling girl, he plunged the needle into her left upper arm, holding it there while she tried to twist herself free. Within a second or two she ceased struggling; to sag in the big man's grasp.

He let her lurch against the wooden bench and then at a snarl from the other he lifted her up bodily and carried her to the tank. It was full of water, in which the girl was held, her head lolling back beneath the surface.

The man against the pillar knew she was dead.

At the same instant the blind alleys of his mind lit up

with flashes of memory. And suddenly a flash widened into a great, stark light which illuminated every recess of his brain with blinding clarity. For an instant of time the world stood still; and in that instant the past raced back to comingle with the here and now.

He knew the girl was Celeste Ruz. He knew who he was, and what had happened to him. The big, dark girl had refused to betray him. She had paid for her defiant courage. She had died in vain. But she had died for him.

He stood there rigid, his spine forced against the pillar, the cords which bound his wrists biting into the flash. The sleek, dark man had carefully put the hypodermic back into its leather case, and slipped it into his pocket. Each movement was calculatedly casual, the expression on his face was calm, smug almost. He eyed him, a bitter, icy smile touching the corners of his mouth; and the other knew for a certainty that he was looking at Leon Stierlin.

Stierlin moved closer.

"You're beginning to remember?" he said. "You know who I am, who you are, why you are here?"

"Yes," he said, "I know who I am."

Chapter Sixteen

"MISS FRAYLE?" the voice had said again, the tone quiet; and the owner of the voice had been a man.

He wore a fawn suit and a brown soft hat. He was of medium height and build and Miss Frayle thought that he looked neither smart nor untidy. He was the sort of nondescript figure unnoticeable in a crowd, unlikely to be the focus of attention. There was a feminine quality about the line of his jaw; his skin appeared soft and as if he had no need to shave. He might have been aged from anything between thirty and fifty. There was a faint greenish glow about his face as if it reflected the colour and atmosphere of the Snake House.

The small, sharp eyes took in her appearance as they darted all over her from under the brim of his hat.

"Yes," she had heard herself say, and was annoyed that her voice sounded so unsteady. "I am Miss Frayle."

She had felt rather than saw the cobra in the glass case behind her move and slither away from its flattened position and she was overcome by a horrible nausea. She had pulled herself together with a tremendous effort of will.

"I thought I could rely on you to come."

"Where is Dr. Morelle?"

The thin smile that had spread across his lips suddenly vanished. "You told no one?" he whispered urgently.

"No one," she said, wondering why he was suddenly anxious.

"We can't talk here," he said, his gaze fixed beyond her left shoulder, so that she had made as if to turn round to see what it was. His voice stopped her. "Do not look round." His accent was slight. "Move on. It will be safer if we do not remain together now. Meet me this afternoon, the Café Anker in Hafenstrasse, the other side of the river. Through the Elbetunnel. Three o'clock."

He had gone; it was as if he had disintegrated in the cool, weed-smelling atmosphere. She had been about to go after him, puzzled and disappointed by his extraordinary behaviour. She remembered his fixed stare over her shoulder. She turned at once to see a familiar, chunky figure in a light suit and soft hat strolling towards her. She gave a casual glance at her watch, the time was ten minutes past twelve.

He must have witnessed her meeting with the man who had gone. Had he been following her all the time? Miss Frayle had no time to sort out the rush of questions that leaped about her mind; he was standing beside her, raising his hat.

"Hello, Miss Frayle," he had said to her pleasantly. "I wondered if by any chance I should see you here." His expression was bland, his blue eyes guileless. "I had to call unexpectedly. Just a routine matter, nothing important."

"I was hoping you had come to find me specially," she managed to say. "With news about Dr. Morelle." She had congratulated herself upon the bold manner in which she had reacted to his sudden appearance, for which she had been totally unprepared. All the same she hoped he could not hear the thumping of her heart, which was racing again.

"I am sorry there is nothing further," he said. "But I hope you have not been disappointed with your visit here?"

"On the contrary, I've found it most interesting."

Her mind had worked furiously in search of suitable answers to the questions she knew must follow. She was convinced that Kriminalinspektor Graap's arrival and their meeting was by no means casual or accidental. He was keeping an eye on her. But did he suspect that she was in contact with someone who knew Dr. Morelle's whereabouts?

"I am so glad," he was saying. His gaze fixed on her; she thought his eyes were the bluest she had ever seen, and the whites of them clear and bright. "And you made a friend?" She contrived to look wide-eyed behind her horn-rims. "The man you were speaking to?" he said. "Was he someone you know?"

Miss Frayle shook her head and looked as if she realized now what he was getting at. Pleasurably surprised at the controlled casualness of her own voice she said: "He asked the way out. He would have to pick on a foreigner." She even gave a giggle at the ludicrous idea of it; but she slyly observed that he appeared to accept her story. Come to think of it, she had reflected somewhat idly, it was odd how often people did stop and ask her to direct them somewhere, when she was in a place which was equally strange to her. She supposed it was something about her face that made her look the helpful type. It always depressed her slightly.

"It will soon be lunch-time," the other had said. "Do you plan to have something here?"

"No, I am going back to the hotel."

"Would you like me to take you? I have a car."

"I shall be certain of not losing my way," she'd smiled at him. She wished he had let her go on alone; all the time he was with her she would have to keep up some conversation, while watching out for any traps he might set her. The effort of coping with this was bound to make her forget the address the man had hurriedly given her. Café Anker, that was it.

On the way back in the black Mercedes-Benz she fought a mental battle in an effort to remember the name, while the other talked about Dr. Morelle and offered various reasons why no news of him had yet come through. At one moment she thought he was making her talk to him with the deliberate object of driving the name out of her head. However, she dismissed the idea as ludicrous, after all the blessed man wasn't a mind-reader.

"I will keep in touch with you Miss Frayle," he said, when they stood in the hotel-foyer. "I shall of course telephone you the moment there is any news."

As soon as he had gone Miss Frayle went to the reception desk and asked for something to write on. She placed the sheet of hotel notepaper on the blotting-pad and wrote down Café Anker. She was sure that was the name the man had said. But what was the name of the street? Something beginning with H? She frowned to herself as she concentrated, trying to hear that quiet voice again.

Hafenstrasse, was that what he'd said? She thought it was and scribbled it down. She folded the paper and slipped it into her handbag. Three o'clock, that was the time.

Hafenstrasse, yes, that was the name of the street, she was sure of it now. On the other side of the river. She took the lift to the second floor and hurried along to her room to fix her face before lunch. She remembered that the man had said something about the Elbetunnel. That meant she'd have to cross the river, obviously, by a tunnel. It seemed straightforward enough. She could check with that helpful man in blue uniform after lunch.

She took half-an-hour over lunch; and it was just after two o'clock when she was back in the foyer. She had skipped through lunch, really too excited to eat, but now she was preparing to set off for the second appointment, she was reluctant to leave the hotel until the last minute in case there might be news of Dr. Morelle. She was reminding herself of the way the man in the Snake House had panicked when he had seen the detective approaching, which indicated that he was hardly likely to be a law-abiding citizen, when she saw a certain amount of danger in asking the way to the address he had given her.

Supposing Kriminalinspektor Graap showed up at the hotel, and the man behind the Reception happened to mention to him that she had been making inquiries about this café? Blue-eyes wouldn't take long to put *zwei* and *zwei* together, she told herself. And if he butted in a second time—she was certain he had followed her to Hagenbeck's Tierpark—he would scare off the man she was going to see for good and all. If he panicked again he would certainly decide that she was working with the detective to lure him into a trap.

These thoughts uppermost, she went out of the hotel, deciding not to ask someone in the street the direction to the Elbetunnel. She started to ask a taxi-cab-driver on the rank outside, then changed her mind. He might also give her away if the police made inquiries about her.

She started walking.

Soon she was in the Gänsemarkt, a square enclosed by buildings which were mostly newspaper offices; and deciding she had sufficiently covered her tracks, she hailed a taxi, a rather decrepit-looking Opel, black with a white stripe round; at the wheel was a walrus-moustached old man, smoking a hooked pipe.

"The Elbetunnel," she said to him, and with a grunt he opened the cab-door for her and she got in. The time was two o'clock precisely. She was giving herself plenty of time, she thought. The taxi turned left off the Gänsmarkt and up Valentis Kamp which was full of shoppers looking for bargains in the cheaper shops and multiple stores. It reminded Miss Frayle of a narrower version of Oxford Street. As it reached Karl Muck Platz, Miss Frayle noticed the Musikhalle, its doors posted with bills announcing concerts and orchestras and which had once housed the British Forces Network radio-station; along Holstenwall passing an expanse of grass and trees, with the Museum für Hamburgische Geschichte on the right. Circling the roundabout at Millerntord and down Helgoländer Allee, past a large statue of Bismarck, where Miss Frayle could see the Elbe glimmering below, while far across the other shore lay veiled in haze. She thought she could smell the tangy flavour of the sea. At the bottom of the slight hill, before her, there loomed the large building of St. Pauli Landing Stage.

A little further on she saw the round dome of the entrance to the Elbetunnel, the only tunnel in Hamburg which burrowed underneath the river and up out of the opposite bank via another round-domed lift building at the Freihafen, that part of the harbour which was free of customs duties to transit shipping.

Miss Frayle's taxicab drew into the giant lift for vehicles, there were smaller lifts for pedestrians, and after a few minutes, descended to the tunnel and was speeding along the right-hand lane; cars and lorries were heading past on the left-hand lane, gleaming in the greenish-yellow glow from the overhead lighting.

She had decided to pay off the taxi at the top of Hafenstrasse with the idea of not advertising her arrival at the Café Anker. By suddenly walking into the place alone, she could convey the impression that she had come by car which had dropped her and would be waiting somewhere not too distant for her safe return. If she failed to return the driver of the car would have his instructions.

It wasn't very good, she told herself, but it was the best way she could think up of suggesting to the strange man she was to meet that while she was obeying his warning not to give away her rendezvous, she was securing her retreat in case of need.

She found the Café Anker half-way down a narrow street, most of one side of which was sheds and warehouses. Beyond them she could see the docks spreading themselves in a zig-zag pattern of derricks and ships' superstructures, masts and funnels against the greyish-blue of the afternoon sky.

Blinking nervously behind her horn-rims, Miss Frayle pushed open the half-glazed door and went into the café. A couple of men at the table nearest her studied her; she caught sight of herself in the gilt-edged large wall mirror that was the seedy-looking place's only decoration, apart from the advertisements for cigarettes and the inevitable coca-cola. A dumpy woman behind the counter which ran along the right side, stared at her with critical interest.

The man she was looking for was at a corner table further away from the door. His soft brown hat was on the back of a chair and as he came towards her from the corner she saw that he was bald with the little hair he had cropped close to his skull.

"You are on time," he said with a smile. "Come and sit down." He spoke quietly, in good English.

She sat down, noting that he was careful to place her with her back to the street-door, while he continued to face it. He took out a crumpled packet of Lucky Strikes, which he offered her. She shook her head.

"American," he said invitingly. She shook her head again. "I'll get some coffee."

"I don't want any coffee, either," she said, "this isn't a social occasion, not for me, it isn't. Where is Dr. Morelle?"

He regarded her levelly. "I understand, of course," he said. "I'm coming to that. But we can't sit here unless we order something."

He got up and went over to the dumpy woman and returned with two cups of coffee. He handed one to her, which she put on the table without looking at. She said to him: "Is Dr. Morelle far from here. And why hasn't he sent me any message by you?"

"He has good reasons for lying low," the other said. "Do you take sugar?"

Miss Frayle said she did but she couldn't have cared less at that moment, this delay was setting her nerves on edge. She watched the man go back to the counter to get some sugar. Miss Frayle's attention shifted to the two men who had stood up and went out, calling something to the woman behind the counter. Her mind grappled with this business about the man in the fawn suit and his supposed contact with Dr. Morelle. If Dr. Morelle was all right, why hadn't he shown up or at least got into touch with the police? How did this strange man know where he was, and no one else? Who was the man? A black weight of doubts and fears descended upon her; she began to regret her impulsive acceptance of the warning not to tell the police. Although, she thought, no harm could come to her, here in this café.

The man was back at the table. He sat down and pushed one of the cups of coffee across to her. "I put two pieces of sugar in," he said, and began stirring his own cup. She stirred her coffee absent-mindedly, putting the spoon in the saucer, while he took a gulp. She suddenly realized his eyes were watchful.

"Why hasn't Dr. Morelle told the police where he is?" she said. "He must know they are looking for him."

"So are other people," he answered her cryptically. "Drink your coffee, it'll do you good. Then I'll take you to him."

He drained his cup, and even though his head was bent Miss Frayle could see that he was watching her. She picked up the cup, raising it to her mouth, and still he watched her. She sensed a bow-taut tension between them, and suddenly knew why he was watching; why he was so insistent she should finish the coffee. He'd put something in when he'd gone to get the sugar.

She knew what his game was, now.

She raised the cup, and it needed very little histrionic ability to pretend that it was an accident; she was shaking all over, and her fingers were weak. The cup fell to the floor and shattered and she felt the warm coffee splash her legs.

"I'm so sorry," she murmured weakly. "But I don't feel very well."

His expression darkened; she doubted if she had fooled him. All the same, it was the best thing she could think of; perhaps pretending that she felt ill would give her an opportunity to escape. He put an expression of concern on his face like fitting on a mask.

"We'll get a taxi," he said. "To the nearest doctor."

"Dr. Morelle," she said.

"Of course," he said.

She stood up slowly, gripping the edge of the table, and grimacing as though in pain. He muttered something about telephoning for a taxi, it would be quickest, he said; and she watched him go through the bead curtains across a narrow doorway. As he pulled them back she saw a wall-phone in the gloom. He glanced back at her, and she did her best to appear as if she was about to pass out. As he reached for the telephone and she heard the metallic tinkle of the receiver being lifted, she dashed for the door.

Chapter Seventeen

WINSOME DEANS paced the gilt and pink bedroom.

Maybe it was because it was the first time she'd come into contact with the occupational risks of Leon's racket, that his methods of dealing with his victims had been brought close to her; but she shivered as she tried to imagine what was taking place now in the cellars below.

First the girl. And now the man. She felt sure of one thing, the final outcome for them both. If not now, at this very moment, then later their death was inevitable. This she knew.

She moved out of the bedroom into the dressing-room; in the cabinet by the window was a bottle of bourbon and a glass. She poured herself a shot, and knocked it back in a gulp. She felt a bit better after that. She lit a cigarette and looked out over the garden, her gaze fastening on the boat-house, and then the speedboat waiting at the jetty.

She felt an urge to get away. Away from Leon and the house. She found herself thinking of New York, and the good times she'd had around the old town. She had a mental picture of slipping away, taking the speed-boat and never coming back. The only thing was she didn't even know how to handle the darned boat. And anyway where could she go? She knew no one in Europe. There was no hope struggling on her ownsome, she couldn't land a meal-ticket like Leon without a whole heap of organizing herself, or terrific luck. And the breaks didn't come that easy when you were going it alone, in a strange part of the world.

If only there was someone she could trust, she told herself vaguely; and then she saw a movement on the jetty. It was the heavily-built man with the hat over his eyes. He was bending over the speed-boat's stern. He must have come up out of the cellar, which opened into the boat-house. There was a door she knew built flush to the back of the boat-house, so that unless you knew about it, you would never guess it was there.

The man had shifted round to the bow of the boat now and she could see he was unfastening the warps. He got into the for'ard cockpit and slipped behind the wheel. She heard the motor cough and start up. It ran at low revs, the Venom engine ticking over as the man took the craft slowly round from the jetty and disappeared into the boat-house.

Winsome Deans wondered if Leon would put in an appearance. She felt she was spying, but she was sure she had not been noticed by the man in the boat, he had been too absorbed in what he was doing; it was the intensity of his attitude, the slow, deliberate movements, almost automaton-like which had held her attention.

That, plus the fact she knew he was concerned with the big, dark girl, and now the desperate-looking man, and not to their advantage, she felt positive of that. The engine revved up again, and a few moments later the boat glided out of the boat-house and began to accelerate down-river. The man was at the wheel and he seemed to be pushing something into position in the boat. It looked like a large bundle, she didn't think it had been there before he went into the boat-house. There was still no sign of Leon.

She watched the blue and white speed-boat chug into the stream to vanish behind the shoulder of the steep bank; she waited, listening to the sixteen foot Avenger's steady throb of its Venom engine die away.

She finished the drink, went through the bedroom and along the landing to the head of the stairs. Leon must still be down there. Her thoughts fastened on the image of the man who had gone with him and the big man. What was happening now? Compulsively she pictured the speed-boat with that large bundle which hadn't been there before, and a dreadful icy chill gripped her. She dismissed the idea; she must be out of her mind to imagine anything like that. Here, under her very nose? She knew Leon was no angel, and he might have been mixed up in some dirty work, maybe one or two people had died on his orders. But he wouldn't murder anyone in his own house. He wouldn't foul his own nest.

But the sight of the thing in the speed-boat stayed in her mind's eye.

She was about to start downstairs when she thought she heard the door behind the Japanese screen open. She moved quickly back into the corner, watching the hall. It was Leon. She dodged out of sight. She heard him go into the library and then his footsteps sounded in the hall. For a moment she thought he was coming upstairs and she wondered how best to act so that he wouldn't suspect she was spying on him. She was about to move boldly into sight and descend to the hall, when she heard him at the front door.

He was going out. She went swiftly into the front bedroom facing her and from behind the curtain listened to him open the garage doors. She heard him go into the garage and then he reversed the Mercedes-Benz convertible out on to the drive and drove off. For a few moments she remained behind the curtain staring at the black shiny roof of the car still by the porch in which the strange man had been brought to the house.

Suddenly she knew what she had to do. And if she was going through with it she'd better make it fast. Leon might be back pretty soon; or the man in the speed-boat. She went down the stairs two at a time. Leon had only one servant around, apart from the daily help; a chauffeur-valet type, a German ex-S.S. man. So Leon had told her. He was a heavy-browed character who never appeared unless he was sent for, but hung around in his own room, reading Yank comics and listening to the American Forces Network. So he wouldn't bother her.

She hurried across the hall into the library. Leon had left the door wide open. She saw the whisky bottle and the empty glass on the desk; he had taken a snifter before he'd beat it. She wondered why? He wasn't the sort who needed a drink this time of day to boost his morale. She concentrated her mind on the object of her visit to the library. It was the drawer in the writing-desk by the french-windows she was interested in. She pulled it open and saw the keys on a ring there. One was the duplicate to the cellar door-key. At least she prayed fervently that it was the key. She had once seen Leon put the keys in the drawer after he'd come up from the cellar. There had been a terrific thunderstorm and it was raining stair-rods and he'd had to get to the boat-house to take a look at the Avenger; some engine-trouble or something. And Leon didn't like getting his feet wet.

She took the keys, closed the drawer and went quietly into the hall, listening. The house was silent. The only sound seemed to be the loud thumping of her heart. Then from somewhere came the muffled beat of jazz. The ex-S.S. man was happy. She heard the phone ring upstairs, it sounded as if it was ringing in Leon's office; it was very faint, muffled by the sound-proofed doors. It wasn't coming from the bedroom, she'd left the bedroom door open. It went through her mind that if it was answered she would drop dead with fright. Only Leon ever took any calls on that phone.

But the phone went on ringing. No one answered it. Then it stopped. She waited for a few moments. The muffled jazz still sounded, so the chauffeur-valet hadn't heard the phone. She told herself she must be stark staring mad to be acting this way. Why in hell was she taking any interest in what went on in the cellar? What had it got to do with her? She knew for sure that Leon would come back before she came upstairs again, or the man in the speed-boat would catch her there. She'd always kept her nose clean up till now.

Her full, pretty mouth tightened in a grim line. She went across the hall, lithe and quick as a cat. The key opened the door behind the screen all right.

She left the door ajar behind her as she went down the claustrophobic passage, her high-heels tapping on the concrete and her eyes narrowed against the light-bulbs close to her head.

She found the man tied to the pillar, where Leon Stierlin had left him. The air was cold, dank, and he looked deathly when she switched on the light. He stared at her blinking in the harsh glare after the gloom in which he had been left, a shadowy darkness, alive with the ghastly spectacle he had witnessed in impotent horror that would never be blotted from his mind.

That Stierlin had a similar end in mind for him he was in no doubt. There seemed little he could do about it, the cords cutting into his wrists every time he tried to ease the strain upon his arms wrenched behind him round the pillar was a painful reminder of his help-lessness.

Only his mind was clear, as if the brutal murder of Celeste Ruz had acted as a violent catharsis.

The last time he had seen the dead girl was after the Nord Express had left Bremen, just before the smash. He must have been knocked out, leaving himself, and Celeste Ruz, who had also probably suffered in the train wreck, at the mercy of Stierlin's agent who was tailing them on Rommerque's instructions. Doubtless the agent had come upon him wandering and suffering from shock and amnesia and after removing all means of identifying him had dumped him in some ditch, left for dead, while he went on to deal with the girl and convey her to Stierlin's Hamburg headquarters. As for what had hap-pened to him subsequently, he could recall thumbing a lift on the autobhahn outside Bremen, which had got him to Hamburg. He recalled meeting Eva at the club, how she had tried to help him. He was convinced that her meeting with the man he had last seen removing the tarpaulin-covered body of Celeste Ruz had been acci-dental. Stierlin's agents, must have been on the alert for his appearance in Hamburg; one, the heavily-built man with his features permanently obscured by his hat-brim, had been lucky.

He was trying to estimate what the time was, how long he had been in the cellars; so much had happened within such an overwhelmingly short space of time, that his thoughts crowded his mind like an avalanche. Then the eerie silence of the cellar suddenly broken by the sound of approaching footsteps, then the door opened, the light-switch had been snapped on. Now the tall blonde young woman was eyeing him in the brash light which flooded the place.

"It's okay," she said. "I'm here to do my boy scout routine."

She crossed to him quickly and her fingers began to work on the cord knotted round his wrists.

Chapter Eighteen

MISS FRAYLE fought off the panic that urged her to rush wildly away from the Café Anker. She had to keep calm, she kept telling herself, as she walked briskly, but unhurriedly along the street. There were two or three people about, and her first impulse had been to stop the first person she met and explain that some crook was trying to murder her. Then she realized that even if she could make herself understood, what passer-by would believe her? She would only delay putting as great a distance as possible between herself and the man in the café.

She thought she would be all right if she kept herself as inconspicuous as she could while she moved fast. Her idea was to keep walking until she could get a taxi, or a bus or train to take her back to her hotel, or the nearest police-station, whichever came first, and provided she could tell a German police-station when she saw one. *Polizeli*—something, she imagined was what she should look out for. She wondered if there would be a blue lamp outside.

The dreadful man was following her.

She had thrown a quick glance over her shoulder, and saw him as he came out into the street with a rush. He was about fifty yards away. She was thankful to note he appeared anxious not to draw attention to himself by running after her. He was walking quickly; but he was obviously afraid that if he turned it into a desperate chase, she would call for help and that was the sort of attention he had no desire to attract, either to her or to himself. If she could keep the distance between them and find a taxicab, she would get away.

It was a grim, stark locality; she could hear the hoot of a ship's siren, she caught glimpses of crane gantries. Everywhere about her there were warehouses and other buildings, and that salty-tang of ships and the waterfront lay strongly on the air.

There was no sign of a taxi; only lorries with their tarpaulin-covered loads, and their diesel exhaust-fumes. She kept on, hoping that she was heading in the right direction. If she could find her way back to the tunnel and once arrive at the other end of it, she felt confident she would find a taxi and safety. She was wondering when she would find the street which would take her to the tunnel. She reached the top of Hafenstrasse, where she had paid off the taxi; there wasn't another in sight. Only two narrow streets leading off in the direction she felt sure the tunnel to be; she couldn't remember which one the taxi had brought her along. She thought she caught the sound of a car behind her, and glancing back she was horrified to see the man in the fawn suit had stopped a small van. He was pointing along the street, obviously telling some tale to the driver which would make his overtaking her appear to be a reasonable action.

He got into the van and it started towards her.

Miss Frayle experienced a strangling sensation as if the man already had got his hands round her neck. That wave of panic overtook her again. She had to do something quickly if she wasn't going to be dragged into the approaching van, and she quickened her pace, searching desperately for some way of escape; she reached a turning into a narrow street, and she pivoted quickly and went down it. She heard the van overshoot the turning. There came a squeal of brakes, the jar of tortured gears and she heard it reversing. But she had gained a few precious seconds. She ran faster.

The street was cobbled, with no pavements. It ran down in a slight gradient between offices and warehouses. She reached an archway on her right leading from one block to another beyond it. There was a sudden poverty-stricken, neglected air about the area, and it struck her that it was a bomb-site which no one had ever bothered to re-build. Gaping holes in the brickwork and mounds of rubble. Glassless windows roughly boarded over, and broken-down gates led into yards and loading bays.

The noise of the engine was loud, it seemed to rattle her eardrums as the van, in low gear, charged down the street, and she realized with a racing heart that she had jumped out of the frying-pan into the fire; she had put herself into an even worse position. Not a human being in sight, there would be no one to help her if the man caught her. And he would in the next few seconds, unless a miracle happened. It was then she saw the alley-way.

She turned into it, not knowing where it would lead; if it would end in a brick wall or a wide space which would place her at her pursuer's mercy.

The screech of the van's brakes came to her, the slam of its door, some exclamations, and then running footsteps after her.

She was in a narrow stone-flagged passage between the buildings. The steps of her thin shoes sounded loud, but even louder were the running steps of the man.

He was shouting at her, his breathless excitement thickening his accent. "Come back, Miss Frayle, I am friend. I take you to Dr. Morelle. I help you; come back. Do not run."

She tore on like one possessed. The alley twisted and narrowed so that she thought at any moment she would come to a dead end. In fact, she came to a broken-down gateway leading into a yard of rubble. She turned into it.

She climbed over the rubble heap, catching her high heels and slipping and half-falling. But she kept her feet, though she felt exactly as if she was racing over slippery sea-shore rocks to escape a tide coming in. On the other side the yard continued alongside a low warehouse building with broken windows and a roof that had been partly stripped of its slates. Across the yard, looking for a door or gap, but there was nothing; ahead now she could see the wall across the end of the yard.

It was a dead end.

But there was a way to the first floor of the building, facing her, an iron staircase fixed to the wall steep to a door next to a loading platform. Up she clattered, and through the half-open door at the top. Just inside, she banged against a large, dented oil drum.

The idea flashed through her mind, and pushing her horn-rims more firmly upon her nose, she glanced outside. The man was at the foot of the stairway; his light hat had fallen off in his hurry, his bald head glistened up at her in the dull light, in another moment he would be half-way up the stairs. Quickly she grabbed the drum, rolling it out to the doorway. He stopped and stared at her as she poised the drum at the top. He yelled something at her in German. He crouched there, hands raised as if to ward off the approaching disaster. Then, a desperate shove and it crashed and bounced down at an increasing pace.

She paused at the top, fascinated to see what would happen, gasping from her exertions. But he was no slouch; a second before the drum reached him, the man jumped over the rail to land some ten feet below twisting over on his ankle as he hit the ground and letting out painful curses.

The drum bounced in the yard, but Miss Frayle didn't wait for any more. As the man got up and limped determinedly towards the stairs again, she swung round and dashed into the gloom of the building.

She halted in the semi-darkness for a moment, uncertain which way to go. An inside wall of broken down timber divided the corridor from the main part of the warehouse floor. Through the gaps she could dimly make out bales of cloth, sacking and heaps of straw mixed with rubble that had fallen from the sagging roof. At every step she took the thick dust rose up in choking clouds. The corridor ran in front of her and behind her. Darkness lay before her and at her back. She decided on the unknown ahead.

Hurrying as fast as the state of the floor would allow, with its broken boards and dust-choked holes, she reached the end where the corridor turned. Hidden behind a large crate, she peered back to the oblong patch of light that was the stairway door. She heard the scrape of footsteps ascending the iron stairs. After a moment, the man came into view. He stood undecided, blotting out the light, a dark menacing silhouette as if listening. Miss Frayle remained still. There was no noise apart from the occasional creak of timber and what she realized with a shudder of horror, must be the scurrying of rats.

The black silhouette suddenly moved, and then instead of heading towards her, Miss Frayle saw with a thankful gulp, that he had decided to search the other end of the warehouse first. She moved quietly on into the heavy gloom, following the turn of the corridor and up a flight of broken wooden stairs; several yards further on, she came to another large storage floor. This was illuminated to some extent by the light which seeped through a long horizontal window, its panes cracked and dirt-encrusted where they weren't smashed altogther. Some of the windows had been boarded over and a tarpaulin was hung beneath one great rent in the roof. Everywhere there were packing-cases, battered crates and mounds of straw and sacking, and the corners were shadowy and eerie, filled with dust and the flesh-crawling scuttling of rats.

Ahead, Miss Frayle could see a doorway opening on to another corridor. She set off towards it, driven on by the fear that soon the man must be after her, and equally sooner or later she felt she must come to a way out of the place. At least she had gained time on the man, she might be able to shake him off, especially if she could move quickly, without giving away her presence.

She passed through the doorway into the corridor with three pairs of glassless windows on the outside. They overlooked a great yard filled with rubbish, overgrown with weeds. At first she wondered if she could get out through one of the windows and drop to the ground; but the distance she would have to jump deterred her, and then she saw that the yard was surrounded on all sides by high walls which appeared to be linked to the building she was in. All about her loomed a great mass of warehouses and offices which had now gone to ruin, or were in a state of demolition, too bomb-scarred and crumbled to be re-built. Even if she got down there, she would still be hemmed in.

At the end of the corridor she went through an archway with a stone floor; ahead of her lay floor-space similar to that she had left behind, and on her right a flight of stone steps led upward. She hesitated, uncertain whether to go on at the same level or see if the steps would lead her out of the building altogether. Perhaps to the roof across which she could make her way, until she reached a fire-escape or something down which she could gain the street? She stood there indecisively, listening automatically for the sound of her pursuer, when there came a movement from above.

Looking at her from the steps was a great, hulking shape. It moved down.

Chapter Nineteen

Winsome Deans hadn't spoken as she bent her blonde head over the cord that tied his wrists behind the concrete pillar, and Dr. Morelle felt that any words from him were superfluous. His mind was fully concentrated on his next move the moment he was free. This sudden, entirely unexpected intervention by this tall, purposeful lovely young girl had charged his every nerve and muscle with a new force. But he still had to escape from the place; and where was Stierlin? What of the man who had removed Celeste Ruz's body?

"Jeez, whoever did this certainly made a production of it," the girl behind him muttered through her teeth.

He decided, from her accent and phraseology and his recollection of the description Celeste Ruz had given him, that this must be the young American woman Stierlin had annexed from his one-time partner in crime, Nathan.

Still, he said nothing. His arms ached, his wrists were chafed; he could only will speed and strength into the girl's fingers. There was nothing he could do to help, only attempt to contract the sinews of his wrists a little more, to give the cord more play. His arms wrenched back around the post did not allow him a fraction of an inch more movement.

His eyes ranged calculatingly round the limits of his prison harshly lit by the bare electric bulb. The cellar had a concrete floor, carried on from the underground passage. The pillar to which he was tied was, with the others supporting the roof; there was the bench on which Celeste Ruz had been lying when he had been brought down, and the water tank in which she had been drowned stood in the recess just opposite him. Turning his head from side to side as best he could he could make out only the walls, their depths lost in shadow. His glance moved round once more and focused on the wooden trap in the wall through which the heavily-built man had dragged the body.

It was a handleless door, narrow and ran up from the floor to a height of about five feet, with a thin metal panel down one side on which it appeared to be hinged. Half-way down was a red button, and Dr. Morelle decided that the trap worked electrically at the press of the button. He wondered where it led to. His speculations were interrupted by a flow of four-letter words from the girl behind him. "This is ruining my nails; but I'll do it if it kills me."

"We shall both be killed, if you don't," he said. His voice was a humourless rasp.

"You don't have to draw me any diagrams," she rapped back.

She worked at the knotted cord furiously. He eyed the door and sniffed the air, deciding that the cellar was located in the region of a river or harbour; there was a dankness that even the walls and concrete failed to exclude which unmistakably indicated the proximity of water. He wondered if that would be his best way out. If there was a boat of some kind which he could take.

There came another bitter outburst of obscenities in

his ear which broke off in a sudden exclamation of triumph. "We finally made it," the girl said. A quick vicious tug which sent needles of pain shooting up his arms and then the pain on his raw wrists relaxed; in a moment his hands were free, and with a grateful murmur Dr. Morelle brought his arms round in front of him, flexing the agonizing stiffness out of his muscles.

"I'm Winsome Deans," she was saying. "Don't ask me why I'm doing this, just get going. And make it real speedy."

"Which way?"

She was already at the trap-door and pressing the button. There was a faint whirring sound and the door began to swing gently back.

"I'd rather you ran the risk of running into that stooge," she said over her shoulder, "than it should be Leon."

The doorway revealed a dark narrow tunnel. It was big enough for a man bending to proceed along. He had been right about the place being in the vicinity of water; the dampness came up out of the tunnel strongly.

"I guess it leads to the boat-house," the girl said. "That big ape went that way——" She broke off and stared at him, her dark-lashed eyes wide. She was suddenly remembering. She was remembering too much. "The girl," she said. "The big, dark one?"

"Celeste Ruz?"

"Wouldn't know her name, it means nothing to me. She was here, Leon brought her."

"He murdered her. I watched him do it."

Her pretty mouth opened; her teeth gleamed white; and then he saw the perspiration beading her upper lip.

She swallowed; she didn't say anything. She turned her face away, as if too ashamed to look at him. She looked at the trap-door entrance. He saw the lovely line of her profile, and it bothered him that anyone so lovely to look at could have become what she was, the kept woman of a deadly monster. She turned back to him, as he said :

"What about you? You'll be in danger."

"I've been crazy like a fool," she said. "What bit me is something I'll never know. I should have my head examined." She drew a deep breath. Her magnificent breasts swelled beneath her tightly-fitting dress. "I guess all I can do now is tag along *avec vous*—that's French for let's get the hell out of here."

He nodded and moved towards the tunnel entrance. "You think there'll be a boat there?"

"Leon's got two; the other bastard took one. That leaves one for us." She gave him a narrowed glance. "You okay? You look like you'd had yourself quite a ball."

He smiled at her, and indicated that she was to go first. He felt like death; he was trembling in every fibre, his legs ached as if he had walked a thousand miles; his arms were burning in their sockets. But his brain was clear enough, the fog and confusion which had choked it from the moment of that thunderous crash on the Nord Express when everything had suddenly blacked-out, had given place to a steely grip of the situation and cold resolution.

He wished he had a gun; it would have come in useful if they encountered the man returning from depositing poor Celeste Ruz in a watery grave, or if Stierlin caught up with them.

He had a sudden thought and was about to speak to the girl, but she was ahead of him, anxious to find the way to the boat-house.

Dr. Morelle followed her, the chill damp atmosphere striking his lungs, so that he coughed harshly. What he was thinking was that if Stierlin was to have the tables turned on him and was to be caught at last and brought to justice, this wasn't the way to go about it.

"I guess this does lead to the boat-house," the girl was saying.

The door had closed behind them. He had seen another metal strip and a button on the other side of the door and the girl had pressed it; the door had swung silently shut again.

He had to stoop as he followed closely on her spike-heels. The floor of the passage went down at a slight gradient, and its surface was of hard clay. The wall and the ceiling dripped with water. In places the sides had been shored-up with stout wooden timbers and planks fastened lengthways between them. In places the height of the ceiling dropped so low that it was necessary for them both to bend almost double. At the base of the decline and where the gradient began to climb upwards again planks had been laid over a pool of water.

This was about the half-way mark, because once they were climbing Dr. Morelle noticed a faint current of fresh air which grew stronger. Now the girl's slim-hipped figure was silhouetted against a glimmer of daylight ahead. The incline ended beneath a square grating, the size of a street man-hole. Reaching up to it was an iron ladder fixed to the wall. Dr. Morelle caught the lap of water, and he guessed they were under the boat-house.

He went up the ladder first. He thrust his fingers into the grating and pushed upward. The iron hatch was light and he pushed it noiselessly away from the hatchway and stepped out on to the floor. Then he bent down and took the girl's hands and helped her up beside him. She glanced back at the opening.

"How about if we replaced the lid," she said, "and dumped something real heavy on it. In case anyone comes looking for us?"

Dr. Morelle knew he had to tell her now. He couldn't force her to listen to him, but he must try and persuade her that it was the right thing to do, otherwise Stierlin would slip through the fingers of the police, just when there was every chance of trapping him.

"I owe everything to you," he said, "and it makes no difference whatever it was that prompted you to do what you did. But if you come with me now, Stierlin will know his game is up and vanish. If you stay to bluff him we shall have him at last——"

"So what?" she cut in. "What's it to you? Are you a cop?"

"My name is Dr. Morelle," he said.

"What, a doc who's a police spy?"

"Something like that," he said, a bleak smile flitting across the corners of his mouth.

She was staring at him curiously. "I don't dig it," she said. "You want me to go back—but he'll know I helped you make your getaway."

"You can bluff him. The mere fact that you didn't come with me will be proof you didn't help me."

"You know what you're asking me? To go back and stick my neck out for the chopper."

"He's a murderer, you know that, now. You owe it to yourself to see him caught."

"Why? He's never done me any harm."

"Supposing he changes his mind? How do you think he'll deal with you then?"

"Who the hell are you, at that? Why are you mixed up in this caper, anyway? You'd do better at home handing out medicine."

"I am helping to cure a great evil," he said.

She was staring at him again, her eyes wide and warm, her mouth a little open. She stepped towards him and put her hand on his arm. "You're the doctor," she said softly. "If I can get back to the house before Leon knows about this, then I can fool him. That's for sure."

"You're pretty wonderful," he said.

"Will you put that in writing?"

"You can rest assured I will do my utmost to secure your future welfare and happiness."

"I believe you could, too," she said.

The implication in her tone was unmistakable, but he responded with a wry twist of an eyebrow. They were on the concrete stage, built against three sides of the boat-house. He turned away from her, his gaze searching the water beyond. There was no sign of the man with the hat-brim over his eyes. So far as Dr. Morelle could see the stretch of river was empty.

"So I'd better beat it back," she was saying.

He was looking across the U-shaped inlet of water to where the streamlined hull of a motor-boat lay, lightly moored fore and aft to the landing-stage posts.

He was trying to convince himself that he was doing the right thing, sending her back to the house. His mind flashed back with pictures of the inert shape in the shadows of the Blue Mosque on Al Raschid Street; and then he was seeing again Stierlin himself driving the hypodermic into Celeste Ruz. This was the sort of death the girl beside him might meet. And it would be he who had sent her to it. She would come with him, or go back; whatever he said she would do. She stood very close to him. He didn't turn to her. He moved away and said it casually over his shoulder.

"Better get back now."

"Okay," he heard her say. "You coming back for me soon?"

"You'll be all right."

"So long, Doc."

He listened to her going down the ladder, then her hurrying footsteps died away along the tunnel. He was trembling all over as he went swiftly round the landing-stage to the boat.

It was a matter of seconds to slip the warps each end and then he stood in the forward cockpit and took the wheel.

He found the ignition switch and pressed the starter. A low hum swelled into a throaty rhythm behind him, and he pushed the gear-lever forward, gently opening the throttle. The next moment he was gliding clear of the landing stage out to the open Elbe.

Without looking back he roared off in the direction of Hamburg.

Chapter Twenty

MISS FRAYLE'S first reaction was that it was some enormous ape, and her mind flew to Hagenbeck's Zoo. Had it escaped from there? Then, as the thumping of her heart lessened she saw that it was a man. He had a massive stomach which shook and quivered as he came down the stone stairs, with a bloated face, black with stubble; his hair was a matted black crow's nest that spilled over his ears and the sides of his face. His clothes were filthy, the trousers were torn and patched, the jacket threadbare, too small for his vast bulk from which his naked arms protruded at the elbows. There was no collar to the rag of a shirt that was open to the waist revealing a mat of black hair from chest to navel.

As he approached, an awful stench preceded him, a sickening odour of beer, dirt and sweat. His face cracked in a grin so that she could see the yellow, broken teeth. She was trying to decide what was best for her to do; behind her was the man from the Café Anker, murderously tracking her down; and here was this dreadful creature, barring her way of escape. Should she turn back and hope to find another way out of the trap? The ape-like figure seemed to be yards away while she paused indecisively, and then suddenly his great hands shot out and grabbed her so that she cried out in pain as his fingers sank into her shoulders. He turned and dragged her along the corridor ahead, kicked open a door rotting on its hinges and she found herself in a large space, with the dim shapes of machinery against the shadowed far wall, the foreground littered with food tins and two heaps of straw covered with blankets. On one crouched a smaller replica of the man who now held her, who raised himself as they entered, his eyes alight with a leer. He swung his bare feet to the floor and stood up in his ragged trousers, tied up with a piece of string around the waist and a dirty shirt, the tail of which flapped behind him. As he moved the black shape of a rat shot from out of the straw bed and he cursed in German and threw a tin after it. The tin rattled away into the gloom.

These were two dockland scavengers, worse than the rats with which they lived, and the man holding her pushed her so that she fell across the nearest straw bed. Her handbag which she had clutched all the way from the Café Anker, fell to the floor and he grabbed it and began to empty the contents, snatching at the money, and her gilt compact which glittered up at him. At the same moment the other threw himself at Miss Frayle, grunting in German. She screamed and for a moment the man drew back from her, his stubble-covered chin dropping with surprise. It was as if he thought she was there of her own accord.

"Don't you touch me," Miss Frayle gasped, taking advantage of his bewilderment. "I'm English—English, do you understand?"

A paroxysm of fear and indignation filled her with blind courage. "Keep your dirty German hands off me, or I'll call the police."

The man backed away momentarily. The other threw

the handbag aside and muttering curses, shoved his companion violently away. In the ensuing struggle between the pair Miss Frayle dashed for the doorway.

But her trembling legs seemed unable to support her; the doorway could have been a mile away. She stumbled and fell headlong, saving her glasses from shooting from her nose only by a quick grab at them. As she sprawled there in a cloud of choking dust and pushed the horn-rims back into place, the big man threw the other aside and with a savage lunge fell on her.

Her scream was cut off as the weight of his gross body winded her. She tried to wriggle from underneath him, but he hugged her close in his huge arms, the appalling stench of him making her feel sick and faint. More weight suddenly pressed down upon her as the smaller man threw himself at the other and struggled to drag him away. The big man was forced to release his embrace which pinioned her, in order to deal with this new attack, and as he turned she slipped from underneath him, crawling quickly out of his reach. She staggered to her feet, with the animal-like sounds of the struggle behind her, and as she started for the doorway, a figure appeared there.

It was her pursuer from the Café Anker.

He dashed in, shouting in German, and Miss Frayle dodged aside. The effect of this newcomer on the scene was magical, though not in the way he had intended; the struggling pair at once broke off, glared at the other man like a couple of bulls sizing up the matador in the bull-ring, and then charged him. Miss Frayle with a muttered prayer of thankfulness gathered all her strength and raced once more for the doorway. From the corner

of her eye she saw the trio engaged in the confusion of
battle; grunts and German curses.

She almost fell into the corridor, turned left, saw the
stone stairs down which the monster had appeared at
her and shot up them. A few yards along from the stairs
she saw an opening in the wall, through which the afternoon sunlight streamed. She raced to it and leaned
against the wall, looking out and getting back her berath.
A rusty, jagged arm of a hoist protruded from the wall
overhead, and a length of chain hung from it. By leaning
out she thought she might catch hold of it, and the idea
struck her that she could lower herself hand over hand
down it to the ground. She glanced down; the chain
stopped short several feet from the ground, so that she
would have quite a tricky drop to make. In any case, the
thought of reaching out brought on an attack of dizzi-
ness, and she decided to continue along this corridor.
There must be another way down, she reassured herself.

She thought she heard shouts from the men down below, and then ran for it lightly and as noiselessly as she
could. The corridor turned at right-angles and she paused.
It was very dark, but she could make out what might be
the head of a staircase; with a glance behind her to reassure herself that none of the monstrous trio she had so
far eluded had put in an appearance, she sped towards
her objective.

There was a flight of stone stairs with an iron rail,
similar to the one she had hurried up, leading to the floor
below. This was the same floor where she had left the
three men and she hesitated, wondering if she was heading back towards them. But it seemed to her that she was

now on the other side of the building; and that she was more likely to find a way out of the vast ramshackle place if she could get to the ground floor than by climbing upward. While she had been urged upwards by the hope that she would be able to make her way across the rooftops in the vicinity, she now gave up the notion. Get back to firm ground, that was what she had to do. Besides, she argued, her pursuers, when they had sorted themselves out from their fighting, would guess she had dashed up the stone stairs and go after her. They might reason that she would not take the next lot of stairs down again.

Hurrying as silently as she could, the only sound the inevitable, spine-freezing scraping of rats, she found another stone staircase to the ground floor. She went down it; she felt convinced she was heading for a way out. She was in a dark space, cluttered with crates and packing-cases, and she edged her way through the dust-filled shadows diagonally across the building. Suddenly she saw a glimmer of light. It looked like a doorway in the wall, half-boarded over.

She gained it and stood breathing raspingly. Through the planks across the doorway she saw a weed-infested path. It led between two long, desolate buildings. She frowned to herself as she adjusted her horn-rims. She hadn't the faintest idea of the lay-out of her surroundings. She failed to recall seeing this part of the building before; but the route she had taken since her headlong dash from Hafenstrasse and that horrible man with his poisoned coffee, had been in somewhat panic-stricken circumstances. She might easily have not seen where she was going.

She pushed against one of the planks on the outside of the doorway. It creaked as the rusted nails holding it gave to the pressure she exerted against it. She pushed again, harder; the nails squeaked more loudly. She turned her shoulder and rammed it against the plank with such force that the plank swung back on the hinge of the nails holding it at one end, so that she nearly shot through the doorway. She recovered herself. The noise had sounded in her ears like the crack of doom.

She was out of the maze of terror that the evilly dark building represented in her desperate mind and was running along the wide path between the two buildings across from the doorway.

She ran to where the weeds and pot-holes turned at the end alongside a high wooden fence. She had thought it must lead to the street, but when she turned at the fence, the remains of a collapsed building adjoining the warehouse blocked the way. The path disappeared under a huge pile of broken masonry. She was positive that the row she had made breaking out through the doorway must have attracted the attention of the men in the building. They would come running; or whoever was left victor of the struggle would.

She stood there in frenzied disappointment; then another look at the heap of rubbish decided her to attempt to reach the fence over it. She lost both her shoes as she picked her painful way through jagged bricks and masonry; her stockings were in ribbons but she set her teeth and clambered on over stone slabs and twisted lengths of iron that moved under her weight in the mortar dust. After a breathless struggle she found herself clutching the top of the fence.

She could just look over the top. The drop was ten feet to the street below. With a final glance back to see that no one was on her heels, she jumped up and folded herself over the top of the fence, balanced see-saw like, her legs kicking behind her, and her hair in her eyes.

The thought came to her irresistibly as she poised there uncertainly : what would Dr. Morelle think if he could see her now?

She managed to get a grip on the fence and swung herself round so that she could get her legs over. Now, she lowered herself as far as she could, then let go. She hit the ground heavily, and fell sideways, but she was unhurt.

It was not until she got to her feet and gave a look up and down that she realized she was in Hafenstrasse. To her right, some twenty yards away she saw the Café Anker.

It was a full circle; she was back where the chase had begun. She spun round to dash the other way; it was an instinctive reaction. She dare not attempt to pass the café, in case friends of the man from whom she had run away should see her. But as she took the first step she saw the man in the fawn suit appear on the street, as if he had walked calmly out of the building from which with such desperate effort she had only just contrived to escape.

He stood there staring at her. His bald head gleaming in a wedge of light that shafted across the street between two buildings. A ship's siren mocked her with a long, mournful note. She noted abstractedly that the man's suit was no longer light coloured, but dusty and stained. He held his hands out in front of him, as if they, too, were filthy as he came with a kind of unhurried speed towards her.

She had no choice. She had to get past the café.

Miss Frayle ran, tears of mortification and fear streaming down her face. She forced her weary limbs into action, but she knew she was at the end of her tether. Any minute she would drop from sheer exhaustion.

Her misted horn-rims obscured the sight of the car that was drawn up outside the Café Anker. She had not noticed it before, in her bitter disappointment after climbing the fence.

Now as she reached the café and called on all her strength to get her past it and run on to the top of Hafenstrasse, where she might find safety, she saw that the car was a black Mercedes-Benz. There was something vaguely familiar about it; something that was sinister, she felt sure of that.

She was past the door of the café; and then as she felt she still had a chance to make it, a figure came out and grasped her by the arm.

She gave a sharp scream as she was swung round, to stare incredulously into the familiarly sardonic face of Dr. Morelle.

Chapter Twenty-One

D<small>R</small>. M<small>ORELLE</small> had opened the throttle and saw the bows lift and felt the stern sink lower in the water as the motor-boat skimmed the Elbe's surface. Spray feathered across the curved windshield which was streamlined into the topsides of the hull, and a white wake streamed astern. A slight touch on the wheel brought the boat's head round and she started off course to begin a wide sweep which another move of the finger soon corrected.

Dr. Morelle had eased the speed a trifle. He kept his eyes skinned for the nearest likely landing-stage on the near bank. He needed to get a taxi into the city as soon as possible. He kept the boat on for another ten minutes before rounding a bend to see a landing-stage with what looked like a garage fronting the road beyond.

He throttled back and steered in towards the stage. He shut the throttle right down and twisted the wheel; as he swung round he pulled the gear-lever back, hoping it would engage reverse. He accelerated again and the boat stopped and began to move slowly backwards. He disengaged the gear and reached for one of the fenders hanging from the end of the stage. He switched off and pulled the boat in with his hands, stepped out and tied up.

He moved swiftly towards the back of the long low building. Following the path round the side he gained the concrete apron of the garage. As he crossed to the office, a young man came out of it and greeted him politely; Dr. Morelle spoke to him crisply in German. The other's expression became alert. He called out and another man in a peaked cap appeared from behind a car in the garage.

"Where do you wish to go?" he asked Dr. Morelle.

"Hamburg *Polizeiwache*." Dr. Morelle said.

A flicker of surprise passed across both men's faces; then the second man gave a nod and darted back into the garage. A couple of minutes later Dr. Morelle was being driven in a fast two-seater Porsche. The young man could drive; he was proud of his car and it could certainly go.

It was a few minutes to four when they pulled into the kerb outside police headquarters. Dr. Morelle thrust some money into the hand of the man at the wheel and went swiftly into the building.

"Dr. Morelle——?"

The eyes of the uniformed policeman on duty which had first regarded him with dubious suspicion, widened. In a flash the man was grinning broadly and he had picked up the desk-telephone.

Dr. Morelle had got no further than the first drag at the cigarette the policeman had offered him, when a chunky, blond man was rushing towards him. "I am Kriminalinspektor Graap. Where have you come from Herr Doktor?"

"A large white house on a corner just outside Hamburg on the way to Blankenese," Dr. Morelle said promptly. He saw the electric clock above the desk. It was precisely fifteen hundred hours.

"What day is it?"

M

The detective frowned at him for a moment, uncomprehendingly. Then he pulled himself together. *"Freitag,"* he said.

Friday.

He had left Paris on the Nord Express on Wednesday evening. It was an eternity ago. A procession of incidents and images started across the screen of Dr. Morelle's mind. The hotels at which he had stayed if only briefly; the glasses of lager with which he had slaked his terrible thirst; the wanderings that had taken him into St. Pauli.

Now Graap was asking him questions and as Dr. Morelle proceeded to put the other in the picture, the detective's bright blue eyes slitted, his mouth tightened. Then he was rapping out orders to the policeman at the desk, who picked up the telephone and began speaking with equal incisiveness.

Dr. Morelle knew that squads of uniformed officers and plain-clothes detectives were already racing by radio-controlled cars to the house where not long ago he had been held captive. His thoughts sped to the girl, Winsome Deans. For a moment he failed to catch something Graap was saying to him.

"Your secretary, Dr. Morelle," the other said again, "Miss Frayle, arrived last night."

Dr. Morelle's expression lightened with a faint amusement. "I'm not surprised," he said with a shrug. "She would be much better employed with the work she has at Harley Street."

"Miss Frayle is staying at the Hotel Vier Jahreseiten," the detective offered.

"In that case, she will be enjoying a restful little holiday." Dr. Morelle gave a heartfelt sigh through a cloud of cigarette smoke. Recalling the work upon which he had left her engaged, the correlation of notes and case-histories concerning a certain psycho-therapeutic investigation, he was forced to reflect wryly that his own case indicating amnesia following upon concussion as a result of the train-crash would prove a not uninteresting study for his files.

A shadow suddenly passed over Kriminalinspektor Graap's face. "I think perhaps we might call there," he said.

Dr. Morelle caught the intonation in the other's voice, but he made no comment, asked no questions. He and the detective went out quickly to the black Mercedes which was waiting. As they drove fast to the Vier Jahreseiten, Graap explained to Dr. Morelle what it was which had prompted his suggestion that they should find Miss Frayle. "She has been deeply concerned about you, Dr. Morelle, as you can imagine. I must confess I shall enjoy the sight of her reaction when you walk in unannounced and confront her. If she is there," he had added almost in an undertone.

The police-car whipped through Hamburg's afternoon traffic to the Vier Jahreseiten, and the detective hurried after Dr. Morelle, moving with long raking strides into the hotel. The man in blue uniform behind Reception looked a little askance at the tall, gaunt, somewhat dishevelled figure; but he promptly telephoned Miss Frayle's room.

There was no reply.

"I thought I saw Miss Frayle go out after lunch," the young man said. "I haven't seen her come back."

"What time was that?"

"About fourteen-hundred hours."

"Miss Frayle left no message?" Kriminalinspektor Graap said.

The man glanced at him, observed the seriousness of his expression. "When you came in with Miss Frayle, Herr Inspektor, just before lunch, and then you went out, the Fräulein asked for some paper and wrote on it, putting it into her handbag. I am sure she did not leave any message here."

Dr. Morelle's glance ranged over the reception desk and he turned away with the detective; there was a speculative look in his eyes, as he said something to the other. Graap had already informed him about his meeting with Miss Frayle at Hagenbeck's Tierpark. "I should have questioned her more closely about this man," he was saying now as they went out of the hotel to their waiting car. "It occurred to me afterwards that it might have been someone meeting her on the pretext that he had some information about you."

Dr. Morelle said nothing as the car snaked swiftly along Holstenwall, busy with traffic, on the right an expanse of grassland. "More than likely," the detective was continuing, "this was one of Stierlin's agents who would make it a condition of their meeting that Miss Frayle told no one." He gave the saturnine profile beside him a look. "She was so concerned for your safety that she walked into the trap."

He thought that Dr. Morelle appeared unimpressed. He glanced out of the window. The mighty Bismarck statue loomed briefly between the façade of houses along the back-streets which the police-car was traversing. He spoke peremptorily to the driver, who stepped on the gas.

Dr. Morelle's eyes were closed as his thoughts tangled with his meeting with Celeste Ruz on the Nord Express, the story she had told him revealing the truth concerning Rommerque; then there had been the attempt by his agent or Stierlin's, it amounted to the same thing, on her life on the train. Following the crash she must have fallen into the agent's hands again, to be conveyed to Stierlin's house, while he, stripped of all identity, had been left for dead.

And then Eva had been hoodwinked by a Stierlin agent. The man next to him heard him draw in his breath in an agonized hiss as he was seeing again the cold-blooded murder of Celeste Ruz. His mind switched to Winsome Deans and his promise to her that she would come to no harm. He wondered how Graap's police-squads had handled the situation at the white house on the Elbe. Where was Stierlin now; what had taken him away from the place after Celeste Ruz's murder?

They were moving out of the lift into the Elbetunnel; no traffic lay ahead in the lane along which the black police-car was travelling and the speedometer needle shot up, and in a few minutes the driver was turning into Hafenstrasse. Arrived at the Café Anker, Dr. Morelle and Kriminalinspektor Graap found the place empty of customers; Graap proceeded to rap probing questions at the dumpy woman behind the counter.

Yes, she had seen a blonde young woman wearing horn-rimmed glasses.

Yes, she had come in alone.

Yes, a man had been waiting for her and they had

talked together. In English the dumpy woman thought. They hadn't spoken German, she was sure of that.

The woman described the man.

Then there had been something about the coffee; the Fräulein had spilled it. Then she had hurried out. The man had gone after her; he had been telephoning, the woman thought; no she couldn't remember hearing him ask for a number. He must have dialled. So it would have been a local number. But, of course, the dumpy woman wouldn't know all these things. She had her café to run, and anyway she was not in the habit of listening to what a customer might say over the telepone.

It was while the police-car driver was on the café telephone to Hamburg *Polizeiwache*, to advise the squads via radio of Graap's whereabouts, that Dr. Morelle had snapped out an exclamation and moved like lightning out of the café.

Next moment, Miss Frayle was staring up at him, utter disbelief in her dust-begrimed face.

"Dr. Morelle——" she gulped.

"You appear to be in some haste, Miss Frayle." He noted her tangled hair, her torn, dirty dress, her stockings in ribbons, and that she was shoeless. "Are you going somewhere?"

Chapter Twenty-Two

It was about an hour later when Dr. Morelle paid off the taxi outside the house in Rothenbaumchaussee. He had noted the other house which had also been converted into an hotel where he had occupied the second-floor front room the previous night.

The front-door of the house where Eva had her room was open. He went in and stood for a few moments glancing round the hall. This was where he had waited while she had tried to get him a room, before she had taken him to the other house.

There was no one about; there was a tired note of shabbiness in the atmosphere and the smell of ham cooking. He thought of calling out, then he saw the dark-painted staircase and he went up it, his footsteps silent on the worn carpet.

He had left Miss Frayle at the Vier Jahreseiten to have a bath and rest. She had quickly recovered from her fainting attack; and he was recalling the expression on her face at his answer to her question : by what miracle had he traced her to the Café Anker? "When you wrote down the address you left the impression on the blotting-pad underneath," he said.

The man in the fawn suit, dirty and suffering from a swelling under his right eye as a result of his argument with the pair in the warehouse, had tried to get away, but the police-car driver had nabbed him smartly.

He had admitted to being on Stierlin's list of agents. He had telephoned the latter's house at the time when Miss Frayle had made her dash from the café; there had been no reply. The recollection of that part of the man's account of his activities was what brought Dr. Morelle's dark brows together, as he went up the gloomy stairs.

Where had Stierlin gone that first time, when he had left him a prisoner in the cellar, and had he returned to disappear again, taking the American girl with him? There was still no news of either when he had left the Vier Jahreseiten. He paused on the first landing. A short passage lay ahead of him with doors on either side. He had the idea which Eva must have given him that she was on the second floor. Something he thought she had said when she had gone round with him to the other house that his room was on the same floor as hers.

He went on up the stairs. The house was very silent; and then as he reached the next landing he heard soft music from one of the rooms that faced him. It sounded like music from a radio, and he decided it was coming from Eva's room. He went quickly along the passage with its threadbare carpet, its dark paintwork and gloomily-papered walls. At any rate the smell of cooking was less noticeable, although now his nostrils caught the aroma of a cigar. He stopped, wondering if it was from the room from which the radio-music, now a little louder could be heard. Was Eva entertaining some friend?

He went past a door and the cigar-aroma seemed suddenly stronger, and he decided that it was from this room that it came, not the one he was approaching. Outside the dark-painted door he waited for a moment, listening.

All he could hear was the music, a dreamy Viennese waltz. He knocked on the door.

"*Komm,*" a voice said. A young woman's voice.

The radio-music was turned down to a dreamy whisper.

He thought as he turned the door-handle that the last time he had heard that voice he was adrift in the fog of amnesia, a man without an identity. He wondered what the girl would think of him now. He opened the door and went in.

It was a smallish room, the large window opposite the door apparently overlooked the back of the house; there was no noise of the trams which ran down Rothenbaum-chaussee. The curtains were half-closed, but the light from a pink-shaded table-lamp in the corner gave out a warm glow. As he closed the door behind him, Dr. Morelle had the impression of glossy theatrical photographs over the mantelpiece on his right and a brightly-coloured screen which hid the wash-basin; but his attention was taken by the girl lying admidst a heap of silken cushions on the wide divan against the other wall.

"Surprise, Doc?" Winsome Deans smiled up at him.

She had kicked off her spike-heeled shoes and pointed a foot at him so that her skirt fell back from her long, slender legs.

"Where is the other girl?" Dr. Morelle said sharply.

"The kid, Eva? You don't have to give her a thought, honest, you don't."

She swung her legs off the divan with a calculated revelation of a pretty petticoat and patted a place next to her. He remained where he was, a sombre figure, one eyebrow raised at her questioningly.

"Komm," she said, smiling at him mischievously. "Park the old frame and take the weight off your mind." She pouted as he made no move. "Okay," she said, "if it's her you're all steamed up over, I'll tell you where she is."

"Is she safe?" he said.

"Safe? From you, d'you mean?"

"From Stierlin."

Her glance narrowed.

"That is why I'm here," he said. Crisply he told her all that it was necessary for her to know of what he had learned from Kriminalinspektor Graap when he had described to him his encounter with the night-club girl. That she was also one of Stierlin's agents, the detective had not the slightest doubt. She was either too stupid, had been inadequately briefed, or had failed to realize the significance of her coincidental meeting with the very man she should have been on the look-out for; there were any number of factors which could have contributed to her dim-wittedness. The minions of the underworld were no less fallible than police-officers. "It sounds as if she was attracted to you," Graap had suggested with a grin and a shrug of his stocky shoulders "Sex blunts the sensibilities." "You flatter me," Dr. Morelle had said. But he could only agree that the other had hit the mark in his estimation of Eva's role in what had transpired.

"He was dead right she was one of Leon's girls," Winsome Deans interrupted him. "That's how I knew about her." She stretched herself out languorously on the divan again, crossing her legs, her skirt caught back up to her rounded thighs.

She began talking fast, breathlessly, pausing only when Dr. Morelle lit a cigarette for her. It was one he offered her from the packet of some American brand which he produced from his inside jacket-pocket. She held on unnecessarily long to his hand holding the match.

He had lit his own cigarette and returning the packet felt the cold touch of the hammerless Smith and Wesson Centennial, loaded with six .38 cartridges, slung in its soft leather holster under his left armpit. It was by way of a loan from the chunky blond detective, when Dr. Morelle had declared his intention of paying a visit to Eva in person. Concerned that Stierlin had spirited himself and Winsome Deans away and that since she would not suspect that he was aware of the truth about her, the night-club girl would, perhaps unwittingly give him a lead to the hide-out Stierlin might have headed for.

"I don't think much of it," Graap had told him frankly. "But anyway, take a gun."

The girl on the divan was describing to him how after his departure she had hurried back into the house. Leon had not returned and she had decided to take the opportunity to give the place a once-over. "I was alone in the dump, except for that goon downstairs listening to his A.F.N., and I meant to learn all I could and help fix the bastard real good," she said, her eyes brilliantly excited through a puff of cigarette-smoke.

With the aid of a heavy paper-knife she had forced open the sound-proof door of his office, which was as usual locked.

Then she had heard someone come into the house. Scared it was Leon she felt her only chance was to bluff it out. She had gone downstairs preparing a story that she had fallen asleep, and wouldn't know a thing about what had happened in the cellar if he asked her. But it wasn't Leon, it was the heavily-built man with the hat-brim over his eyes.

He had needed a drink after the job he'd done. She gave him a stiff one. He had begun gabbing away to release the tension that knotted him, she hadn't discouraged him; scared as she was that Leon would return, she let him talk. He had come up from the boat-house through the garden. He hadn't come through the cellar so he was unaware of Dr. Morelle's escape; he had told her gloatingly who it was held prisoner there and who was due for his when the boss got back. He hadn't noticed the motor-boat had gone.

Gab, gab; he had told Winsome Deans about the girl, Eva, how the stupid bitch had bumped into this Dr. Morelle right out of the blue and hadn't realized who he was and the danger he spelt with a capital D. Stierlin had been keeping tabs on him ever since he'd arrived in Paris and contacted the *flic*, Rommerque. Yes, the man with the hat-brim had really dredged up plenty about what he knew of the Hamburg end of the racket; he was under the impression all along she was wise to what went on, and the details.

She didn't disillusion him.

"Like taking candy from a baby," Winsome Deans said. The problem was to get rid of him while she made her own getaway. She betted on asking him to take her for a spin in the motor-boat, flirted with him a bit. It had worked. "I got him to put me ashore as soon as I figured I could get a taxi. Pretended I needed the john pronto, what gent could refuse that? I left him waiting in the boat and I beat it."

"What brought you here?" he said.

"A hunch, I guess. I figured you'd want to make with the talk with little Eva again——" She broke off. "That's not strictly levelling with you, Doc," she said through a puff of cigarette-smoke. "You want to know the truth? I'll give it you. Leon is out gunning for this Eva baby; he means to remove her from his list for keeps. That's why he took a powder from the house earlier. He'd been tipped off she'd let the side down; that old hat-brim gave him the good news, and Leon it seems likes to take care of those sort of chores personally. You might call him a sadist, I imagine."

She was talking at a terrific rate again. It was if some compulsion was driving her, that she couldn't stop. She had to go on snapping out the words at him. He had made an involuntary move towards her. She took her cigarette out of her mouth; he could see the gleam of her white teeth as she watched him.

"So I was right," she said. "You were scared for her, you knew she was in danger from him? So you wanted to get here before he did." She smiled at him. "You can relax on that one, Doc. Leon won't come calling; you see, he knows where she is, and nothing you can do can help her now."

"Where is she?" His voice was a deadly whisper.

She shook her head. "It's too late, anyway." She saw his face and shrugged. "Okay, if you really want to know. I found her here, so I told her I'd met up with you and you were crazy to see her, and you were already at a certain little hotel and she was to go there. If you were out, you would soon be back, she was to wait around; you would show for sure."

He didn't say anything, he just stood over her, his face looking as if it had been chiselled from ivory, the perspiration was running down from his greying temples, his eyes were burning into her. She smiled up at him, her soft warm mouth curved back from her teeth.

"So you don't want to know the rest, Doc? So I'll tell you just the same. Before I took off with that stooge in the boat, I went back to Leon's office. I went through it like a whirlwind. I found a list of names and Hamburg phone-numbers; like Eva's name and the Grosse-freiheit club where she worked. And others, where I figured he must check with if he was looking for her."

She broke off to contemplate him with a calm, knowing look. She waited for him to tell her to continue. When he remained silent and still, she pouted. "You want to know what I did about that, Doc? I called every one and said for them to tip off Leon if he contacted them where he would find that dumb bitch. I said for them to tell him she wasn't here—that she'd given this away to the gendarmes." She took a long, deep drag at her cigarette. "He will be certain to have found her by now."

Again that terrible vision filled his brain: Celeste Ruz crumpling beneath the effect of the hypodermic and being pushed unresisting under the water in the tank. He knew that if Stierlin found her he would deal with her as mercilessly.

"The name of the hotel." He bent over her, speaking through his teeth.

"You want it, you come and get it, Doc."

The radio-music all thrilling violins muted and

dreamy; and suddenly she raised herself on the divan and curved her arms round his neck, pulling his face down to hers in a clinging kiss. He tried to tear her white, soft arms from him, but she hung on, whispering inarticulately, covering his mouth, his eyes with kisses. Still clinging to him she threw back her head and gasped: "You want to save her—you think there's still time—you gotta give me what I want first. Come on, Doc—I hold the ace, the only way you can trump it, is —the only way."

Freeing one hand for a moment, she tore at the front of her dress, so that her wonderful breasts curved up at him, and pulled his head down to her. Now she was mouthing words at him in an incoherent flow. Her scent filled his nostrils, her burning animal fervour overwhelmed him; and with a triumphant cry she fell back among the cushions on the divan, dragging him on top of her.

"So you can name it blackmail," she was saying huskily. "It's the sweetest kind of blackmail you'll ever have to pay."

She was trying to rip his coat from his shoulders when the door was flung open.

It was Stierlin who stood there.

He came into the room, heeling the door shut behind him. Dr. Morelle wheeled up and faced him at the same moment that the girl uttered a long moan of abject terror.

"You didn't think it out enough, did you?"

His French accent was thick with murderous fury, as, a quivering, evil figure he spat at the girl. She stood reeling on her feet, her blonde head nodding from side to side like some demented thing. Strange sounds from her half-open mouth, as if the fear that gripped her was spelling out.

"You didn't think she'd talk—before I shut her stupid trap?" Dreadful words from him while he stood poised like some monstrous cat; and then the knife appeared in his hand. "I'll cut your heart out," he hissed.

He made to spring, and then the Smith and Wesson barked.

Stierlin was staring with sagging jaw in surprise at the smoking revolver in Dr. Morelle's hand. He moved forward, and it was Dr. Morelle's turn to narrow his eyes in amazement. He knew he had hit the other; he could see the blood spreading over the whiteness of his shirt below the heart. The .38 was a man-stopper, he knew that.

Yet Stierlin was still coming at him. Suddenly in a paroxysm, the knife flashed.

At the same instant there was a movement beside Dr. Morelle, and then a terrible scream which would echo in his ear for a long time. The knife stuck in Winsome Dean's white, curving throat up to its black hilt.

Dr. Morelle held her as she died; over her head, bent as if weighed down by the glorious blonde hair, he saw Stierlin slowly give at the knees and sink first on his knees and then eyes glassily rolling upwards, fall flat on his face. He had hurled the knife as a reflex-action.

The .38 had stopped him, after all.